Heat

HEAT

A Firefighters of Montana Romance

Karen Foley

TULE
PUBLISHING

CHAPTER ONE

Glacier Creek, MT

THE FIRE BUZZER catapulted him out of bed at dawn, the strident alarm blaring through the firefighting base that housed the Glacier Creek smokejumpers, hotshot team, and search and rescue team. In the dormitory, Tyler Dodson was on his feet and yanking his pants up before he was even fully awake, responding instinctively to years of training.

He'd been back at the base for less than twenty-four hours after jumping a wildfire in Idaho earlier in the week. He'd had just enough time to shower, eat, and hit the sack for some much needed sleep before this next call came in, but he wasn't complaining. He needed the overtime pay if he ever wanted to break ground on the sweet piece of real estate he'd bought over on the north ridge two years ago. He rented a small apartment in Whitefish year-round, but he lived at the smokejumping base during the summer so he wouldn't miss any calls. With the crazy wildfire season they'd been having this summer, it looked like he'd finally have enough money to finance the construction of the timber frame house he'd been dreaming about.

Tyler glanced at his watch as he made his way swiftly out of the dormitory to the ready room. When the fire buzzer sounded, the smokejumpers had just fifteen minutes to suit up and get their asses on the jump plane. He took the stairs leading from the sleeping quarters to the ready room two at a time. As he crossed the lobby, he tried not to look at the parachute that hung from the balcony of the vaulted ceiling, a grim tribute to their former captain.

The outside doors pushed open and Vin Kingston came in, acknowledging Tyler with a nod as Vin fell into step beside him. Tyler had been a mentor to the younger man when Vin had gone through smokejumper training several years earlier. They'd both been close to their former captain, Russ Edwards, although that could be said of most of the team. Russ, with his easygoing nature, made everyone feel as if they'd been friends with him forever. After Russ had been killed in a jump accident the previous year, Tyler had thought Vin might quit the smokejumpers for good. He didn't miss how Vin glanced up at the chute hanging over their heads.

Russ's death had shocked the tightknit firefighting community, but had been especially difficult for Vin; even moreso when Russ's widow, Jacqui, overcome with grief, had abruptly quit Montana and moved to Florida. Vin had surprised everyone by staying on, remote but determined to look after Russ and Jacqui's dog, Muttley. But none of the crew had been surprised when Jacqui returned to Glacier

Creek, thinner and more subdued than they remembered, and eventually succumbed to Vin's charm. Only Tyler knew Vin had had a thing for Jacqui long before she became a widow.

Tyler was glad things had worked out for them. They needed each other, and while Tyler thought Russ and Jacqui had been great together, Vin had confided the marriage hadn't been quite as perfect as they'd all believed. Tyler had to admit Vin and Jacqui made a damn good team. After what they'd both been through, they deserved some happiness.

"Hey, Vin." He greeted the other man. "Any word on what we have?"

"Don't know yet, but I can tell you that Jacqui's not too thrilled about it."

"Oh yeah?" Tyler shot his friend a sideways glance as they made their way to the ready room. "She tell you that?"

Vin snorted. "Nope. You know Jacqui; she'd never say anything about my jumping, but I know she worries every time I get called up."

Jacqui had good reason to worry, considering her first husband had been fatally injured during a jump. Tyler gave the other man a reassuring slap on the shoulder. "I'll make sure you get back in one piece."

He knew as well as Vin what marriage to a smokejumper could do to a woman. That was another thing they had in common—their first marriages had each gone down the shitter. Tyler's marriage—to a girl from California—had lasted for two years, but it had been doomed from the beginning; he'd just been too stubborn to realize it.

Vin, on the other hand, had married a local girl, Tori, but she hadn't been able to handle his long absences during the busy fire season. Vin and Tori still saw each other on a regular basis, since she worked as a waitress at The Drop Zone pub, but they were at least on cordial terms. Tyler hadn't seen or spoken to Alicia in almost eight years, since she'd remarried and popped out a couple of kids.

He pushed the unpleasant memories aside. Ten years might have passed since Alicia had divorced him, but he'd learned his lesson. There would be no more weddings for him.

Most of the smokejumper team had already arrived and were suiting up when Tyler and Vin reached the ready room, where the jumpers had their own equipment lockers and speed racks. The jump gear was pre-positioned to facilitate a swift suit up, and it took less than three minutes for Tyler to pull on his protective gear.

The suit itself was made of Kevlar, heavily padded to provide protection from tree landings and slamming into the ground. The jacket had a high collar to protect his neck and his helmet was equipped with a mesh face guard. He slipped into his harness, which would attach to his parachute, and buckled it securely. Lastly, he grabbed his PG bag, so called because it contained his personal gear, and then he jogged out to the flight line with the rest of the team.

The first glimmers of dawn were spreading pink and gold fingers across the horizon as Tyler made his way across the tarmac toward the waiting plane. Clouds of dust erupted around each man as they dropped their packs in the staging area. Almost immediately, the ground crew began loading the gear into the plane. The packs would be rigged into parachutes, and dropped separately, once the jumpers were safely on the ground.

"Okay, listen up!"

Sam Gaskill, the new captain who had replaced Russ several months earlier, gathered the crew in close for the in-brief. He was a few years younger than Tyler, but had proven his skill, both as a leader and a smokejumper, during this insanely busy fire season. Tyler didn't begrudge the other man his newfound responsibilities as captain, although he knew some of the other crew hadn't completely warmed up to Sam yet. He'd come in from outside the Glacier Creek community, and there were some guys who still complained that they hadn't been selected for the position.

Tyler had thrown his own name into the hat, and had been more than a little surprised that he hadn't made the cut, but he sure as hell wasn't going to whine about it. That kind of shit didn't endear anyone to the brass, and only eroded the crew's ability to work together as a team. And when anyone became more important than the sum of the parts, it usually led to trouble. A smokejumper couldn't operate alone, at least not safely. And Tyler was all about safety. He never wanted to experience another day like the one when they'd lost Russ.

As Sam began to brief the team about the deployment, Tyler noticed two other men standing to one side, listening. One of the men was their new spotter, Doster Cohen. His job was to select the best landing site for the jumpers, close to the fire.

"Hey." Vin nudged him, nodding in Sam's direction. "Isn't that your old man?"

Tyler peered through the near-dawn darkness and recognized the second man standing just behind Captain Gaskill, and nearly groaned.

His old man.

What a joke.

Tyler and Mike Eldridge weren't related by blood, as Mike had made abundantly clear, nearly from the moment he'd married Tyler's mother.

I'm not your father.

How many times had Mike said those words to Tyler? More times than he could count. The first time had been following the wedding ceremony, when Tyler—just five years old—had happily declared that he finally had a dad. Mike Eldridge had crouched down in front of him, looked directly into his eyes, and said, "I'm not your dad, Tyler. You're not to call me that. To you, I'm just Mike."

And that had pretty much summed up their relationship

for the next thirty years. But that hadn't stopped Tyler from trying. He'd done everything he could think of to gain Mike's approval, naively thinking if he could just be smart enough, strong enough, brave enough, then maybe Mike would want him.

He'd hero-worshipped his stepfather.

Mike Eldridge had been part of the Glacier Creek base for almost forty years. In his mid-sixties, he was a granite slab of a man, with a stubborn jaw and eyes like chips of glacial ice. He'd started his career as a hotshot, before moving over to the smokejumpers in his late twenties. He was very nearly a legend in the wildland firefighting world, having jumped more than three hundred fires during his long career. Retired now, he hadn't jumped in almost two decades, and instead taught several wildfire training courses required for hotshot and smokejumper qualification. Tyler had taken them all. He had firsthand knowledge about the kind of man Mike was—hard, uncompromising, and unforgiving.

He and Tyler's biological father had been best friends, part of the Glacier Creek hotshot crew. Bryce Dodson had been killed fighting a wildfire when Tyler was just a toddler; he had no memories of his father. But he'd heard the stories—Bryce Dodsen had been like the wildfires he'd battled—hot, wild, and unpredictable.

Reckless.

Sometimes Tyler wondered if that was why Mike Eldridge was such a hardass with him; he didn't want him growing up to be like his father. But Tyler couldn't recall a time when he didn't want to be a smokejumper. Growing up in the shadow of his stepfather gave him a unique vantage point, and he would have done anything to gain that man's approval. But Mike Eldridge had remained frustratingly aloof, even when Tyler had been voted all-star athlete in high-school; even when he'd enrolled in firefighting courses, and had graduated top in his class, and could hump a sixty-pound pack of gear up the side of a mountain in record time.

He'd gotten nothing.

Okay, there'd been the time right after graduation, when he had been working a summer job with a hotshot crew out of Helena, and they'd deployed to California to fight a wildfire there. Tyler had been twenty-three and pretty full of himself. After containing the fire, the crew had kicked back at a local pub where he'd met Alicia, a pretty blonde with a golden tan, and legs that could wrap around him like a vine. He'd been too dazed from all the sex to realize they weren't a good match in the ways that mattered.

Before he knew it, they were married and living in his tiny, two-room apartment in downtown Whitefish, Montana. Oh, he'd gotten plenty from Mike Eldridge then. He'd thought the older man was going to burst an artery, he'd been so furious with Tyler. He'd called him irresponsible.

Selfish.

Impulsive.

Not the qualities they were looking for in a full-time hotshot. That was when Tyler had known he'd blown it. He'd spent another couple of years working part-time jobs on different hotshot teams, trying to prove his worth. In the meantime, Alicia grew tired of being alone, and had returned to California and filed for divorce. Even knowing it was for the best, it had left a bitter taste in Tyler's mouth. So when he got hired on full-time with the hotshots, and later with the Glacier Creek smokejumpers, he'd put any thoughts of marriage behind him.

He didn't need to go through that again. His crew was his family. And over the next ten years, they *had* become his family. He'd gladly give his life for any of them, even the annoyingly cheerful Marco Linetti, the youngest crew member who had recently made it through boot camp, and was anxious to prove himself.

Tyler dragged his thoughts away from Mike Eldridge, and instead focused on the in-brief, which was thankfully short and sweet. Lightning had spawned a wildfire in the heavily timbered, mountainous terrain of Glacier National Park, on the eastern side of the popular tourist destination. High winds, compounded by a hot, dry summer had quickly fueled the blaze into an inferno that was rapidly devouring everything in its path.

Until now, the local ground crews from Missoula and St. Mary had managed the suppression effort, but shifting winds had caused the fire to behave erratically, jumping fire lines and spawning new fires that quickly grew and spread. The blaze had shut down the eastern portion of the park, and had destroyed thousands of acres of parkland. Fire roads were quickly becoming impassable, and the smokejumpers were the last line of defense before the wildfire threatened the nearby town of St. Mary.

As Tyler jogged toward the plane, he thought he heard Mike call his name, but he didn't look back. He wasn't that same starstruck kid anymore. He no longer needed or wanted Mike's approval.

Once they were airborne, Tyler took time to strap on his parachute and take stock of who he'd be jumping with. There were fifteen jumpers in all, including the new captain. Vin sat beside him, and across from him sat Ace Clark, one of the younger guys.

Tyler had jumped plenty of times with Liam Ferguson, whose sister, Miranda, happened to be their pilot. The two of them had worked out of the Glacier Creek base almost as long as Tyler. Greg Winters and Garrett Broxson, both married, sat toward the front, and would be among the first ones out the door. Greg was a seasonal part-timer, but he was good at his job. Tyler had tried to persuade him to hire on full-time, but Greg insisted his wife would never allow it. The rest of the crew was comprised of guys who Tyler knew well and had jumped with dozens of time. He relaxed fractionally. No rookies on board, which meant he could focus on his own jump without worrying about the others.

Within an hour they were approaching the jump site.

The sun had risen and, looking out the window of the plane, Tyler viewed the billowing black smoke that marred the brilliant sunrise. From his vantage point, he could see a long ridge of mountains topped with flames, and more wildfire extending down the eastern slope, toward the flatlands. He saw the long, narrow finger of St. Mary Lake, and beyond that, the tiny town of St. Mary. Captain Gaskill hadn't been kidding—there were several spot fires along the western tip of the lake, and at least one had spread along the northern shore, in the direction of the town. The pilot made several passes over the front edge of the fire to determine the best spot to drop the crew.

The jump door was open now and the spotter leaned out, scoping out a safe landing site. He pulled several weighted, crepe paper streamers from a basket by the door and dropped them out of the plane, watching to see how they drifted, to ensure they came close to the landing site he had selected.

Doster Cohen was new to the base, and as Tyler glanced at the others, their grim expressions told him they were all thinking the same thing; they were recalling the day that their former captain, Russ Edwards, had died.

The spotter that day had selected a drop point, and released the streamers to ensure an accurate glide. But when Russ jumped, a rogue wind had caught him, driving him into a stand of tall spruces where he'd become tangled. He'd been unconscious, but had no visible injuries. They'd evacuated him by helicopter, convinced he would be okay, so it had been a shock to learn he had died en route to the hospital from massive internal injuries and head trauma.

He'd never regained consciousness.

The spotter had blamed himself, although an investigation had cleared him of any wrongdoing. He'd left the forest service soon afterward.

Tyler worried about wind gusts, not just for himself but for the rest of the guys. He knew the possibility of injury always existed, but he liked to think their attention to safety eliminated most of the risks. He was all about safety, even more so since Russ's accident.

Surveying the landscape below, he saw the drop point where the streamers had landed. The spotter had selected a small tract of meadow on the side of the steep terrain, where the ground was more level. But each jumper would have to hit the spot precisely, since just above the meadow was dense forest, and the ground below fell away to a deep ravine.

While the jumpers made final preparations, Tyler took a moment to look at his map, orienting himself with the terrain, and figuring out how they might reach the leading edge of the blaze quickly, without overtaxing themselves. They'd each haul their own packs and equipment, and while they were all in top physical shape, they'd need all their stamina to battle the wildfire. Looking at the map, Tyler figured they could follow the ridge line horizontally, and avoid exerting too much energy in climbing. He also marked the map with two possible escape routes, in case the fire overwhelmed them and forced them to retreat.

"Hey, Ty." Someone bumped his shoulder, and he looked up to see Sam crouched beside him. "We have a situation. I need you and two other guys to do a structure assessment, and possibly an evacuation. I'll take the others and tackle the front edge of the main fire. I want you to be the point man for the evac."

Tyler felt his eyebrows go up. They didn't typically do evacuations, although it wasn't outside their realm of duties. He bent to take a closer look at the map where Sam was pointing. On the extreme edge of the park, he could see what looked like an access road snaking into the steeper terrain.

"What kind of an evacuation?"

"A man and his daughter. They were told to leave two days ago, but looks like they decided to stay. The landlines are down, and the fire roads are impassable, otherwise the St. Mary crew would go in and get them. They can still use this access road if they leave in the next hour. It'll take the ground crews at least two hours to reach them, which is why they want us to go in. The fire will reach the access road at this point"—Sam jabbed a finger at a spot on the squiggly line—"within an hour. If we can't get them safely beyond this point, we'll be looking at an aerial evac."

Tyler could see the property was directly in the path of the fire. He barely contained a snort of contempt. Although the fire marshals provided ample warning for residents to flee ahead of a wildfire, there were always those who believed they could ride out the storm. They soaked their homes with water and hunkered down, putting their lives at risk, as well as the lives of those trying to rescue them. Tyler would go in after the man and his daughter because that was his job, but that didn't mean he had to like it. He resented risking the safety of his crew because some jack-wagon thought he was fireproof. That the man would endanger his own daughter—a child—was even more infuriating.

"I'll take Vin and Ace," he said. "We'll get these people to safety and cut a fire line here." He indicated a spot ahead of the leading edge of the fire. "If things get dicey, I'll call for a slurry drop."

Slurry was a fire retardant liquid, dropped by aircraft ahead of a wildfire, to protect that area from catching fire. Most commonly, it was used to protect homes and people.

Sam nodded. "They're scooping water out of St. Mary Lake and dumping it along the access road. If they can keep the road wet, those folks will have a good chance of making it down the mountain." He started to move away, and then turned back. "Listen, that front is moving fast and hot. No heroics. Just get those people out, and then you hightail it out of there. Head back to the drop site, and radio me for our position."

Tyler folded his map and tucked it inside his suit, as Sam climbed across the gear to tell Vin, Ace, and Doster about the evac plan. Sam and the spotter bent their heads over the map, debating on where to drop Tyler and the other two jumpers. After several moments, obviously satisfied, Sam gave Doster a slap on the back, and then signaled the remaining men for the first jump. Tyler watched as each man positioned himself in the open door, waited for the spotter to tap him on the leg, and pushed himself out into the open sky.

Then it was just the four of them left in the plane, as the pilot banked sharply and the spotter leaned out of the open door to survey the land beneath them. Tyler never tired of seeing the majestic mountain ranges and sweeping valleys that defined this part of Montana. He'd lived here his entire life, had spent countless days hiking through the wilderness of the national park. Despite having traveled all over the continental U.S. and Canada, he couldn't imagine living anywhere else. Protecting this magnificent land from the ravages of wildfire was both a duty, and a privilege.

Less than five minutes later, they were over the second drop site. Tyler braced himself in the opening of the plane, surveying the area below. The landing site was a mix of conifer trees, meadows, and brush just below a rocky out-crop. If the winds didn't cooperate, there a risk of overshooting the drop site and being pushed into the rocks, or being carried into a dense copse of tall spruce. Either would suck. Tyler had dropped into trees before, and even if he managed to avoid being impaled by a branch, or getting his chute lines tangled, it was a complete drag.

When he felt the slap on his leg, he pushed forward, out of the plane and into the open air, free-falling toward earth. Tyler silently acknowledged he always had some anxiety before jumping, but once he was actually airborne, all of that vanished.

He was flying, free and untethered, the wind whipping at his jumpsuit and pushing at his face, and his heart soared with the sheer thrill of it. Then he pulled his chute and felt himself jerked upward, his downward plummet momentarily suspended. He glanced up to see the bright blue, rectangular canopy open above him. Grasping the two toggle handles, he peered down over his boots to where the ground was swiftly rising up to meet him. He steered toward the landing site, maneuvering himself to the center of the small clearing, and pulled hard on both toggles to slow his approach.

He landed on his feet, and quickly gathered in his chute and stripped off his helmet and his protective gear. Shading his eyes, he watched as Vin and Ace dropped out of the sky, wincing as Ace hit the ground hard. But the younger man was up on his feet almost immediately, and Tyler gave the thumbs up to the spotter, as the plane circled above them. Within minutes, their packs and equipment were dropped out of the aircraft, and Tyler swore softly as one of them drifted too far and landed in the trees. Retrieving the gear would cost them precious minutes and, with the wildfire bearing down on the trapped family, they needed every second.

It took them less than ten minutes to store their chutes, retrieve their gear, and begin hiking toward the threatened property. As they closed in on the wildfire, Tyler could smell burning trees and hear the ominous crackle of flames as the wildfire consumed the dry underbrush and spruce. He glanced at his map.

"We're heading directly toward the fire. The property should be straight ahead, through these trees," he shouted to Vin. "We'll bring the family back this way, and get them to the access road."

As long as the access road was still viable. If things went south and the road was impassable, they would bring them back to the drop site and call in a chopper. He could hear the roar of the wildfire ahead of them, and several times they encountered small fires that had sprung up from stray embers, carried by the wind. They suppressed those flames on the spot, working quickly to clear away flammable debris, and kick dirt over the embers. Sweat soaked Tyler's shirt and ran in rivulets down his neck. His eyes burned from the smoke that filled the air, and he swiped the moisture from his face with the back of his gloved hands. They hadn't even reached the main fire, and already he'd had a good workout.

They continued to push their way through the trees, using their pulaskis and, on one occasion, a chainsaw to cut through the dense forest. The sound of the wildfire grew louder. Through the brush, Tyler could now see the beginning of the property, and what looked like a high, wire fence that ran as far as he could see to either side.

Great. Now, they'd have to cut through the fencing to get to the house. Tyler cursed under his breath. The three men reached the fence line and Tyler stood back, momentarily puzzled. There were actually two wire fences, one inside the other, with a three-foot space separating them.

"What the hell?" Vin peered through the fencing. "Did you see that?"

A dark shadow moved on the other side of the fencing.

"Yeah, looked like a dog," Ace said.

"Ah, hell." Vin swore. "I know where we are. That wasn't a dog—that was a wolf."

Both Tyler and Ace turned to look at him, and Tyler knew his face showed his astonishment.

"I've heard of this place…it's a wolf sanctuary," Vin said, swiping a hand across his eyes. "I just didn't realize it was so far off the beaten path."

Christ. *Wolves.* How many were there? And had their enclosure been compromised by the wildfire? Tyler knew enough about wolves to know they preferred to avoid any contact with humans, but with the wildfire almost on top of them, their behavior could be unpredictable. Dangerous.

Perfect. Just when he thought the situation couldn't get any worse, now he had to worry about wolves.

CHAPTER TWO

W HO WOULD HAVE guessed there were pine trees in hell? An entire forest of them, snapping and crackling as the advancing firestorm consumed them in roaring columns of flame. Overhead, the sky was black with smoke, and chunks of burning ash and debris drifted down all around. The acrid stench of charred aspen and pine filled the air, making it nearly impossible to breathe. No, this wasn't hell; this was something even worse.

Wildfire.

Callie McClain guessed she had less than an hour before the inferno reached the timbered ranch house, and then the outbuildings, and then, heaven help her, the animal enclosures. The thought made her mouth go dry with fear.

How could she have been so stupid? How could she have missed the news reports that the massive wildfire, first spotted more than fifteen miles to the west, had shifted, jumping fire lines and mountain roads to spawn new, separate fires? Why hadn't she bundled her father into the pickup truck two days ago, when the fire marshal had first warned them that evacuation might become necessary?

Because he hadn't been sure they would need to evacuate.

Because she hadn't believed the fire would advance this far, and she'd been reluctant to cause her father any additional distress after his recent heart attack. When she'd first broached the subject of leaving, he'd adamantly refused to discuss the issue. Always the pessimist, Callie had packed a duffel bag of clothing for her dad, as well as a box of photos and his important documents. She'd been living out of a suitcase since flying in from California two weeks earlier, so she was ready to go at a moment's notice.

Over the past two days, her father had become increasingly stubborn. He'd dismissed the wildfire as a threat, convinced it would never reach their property. He'd lived on the edge of Glacier National Park for more than forty years; he'd seen his share of wildfires, and had told her this one would be contained and extinguished well before it reached them.

Callie had believed him.

Now it might be too late. The narrow pass that sliced through the surrounding mountains and connected their property with the main road might be impassable. If that were the case, both she and her father—and his beloved animals—could very well die.

Frank McClain had operated a wolf sanctuary on his steep, mountain property for as long as Callie could recall—since she'd been a child. Presently, there were just five wolf packs living at the sanctuary, twelve wolves in total, but they meant everything to Frank. She was pretty sure he loved those wolves more than he did his only daughter. With the help of Randy, one of the sanctuary volunteers, they had successfully transferred five wolves into the kennel truck, but the remaining seven wolves had retreated to the back of their enclosures, where the terrain was steep and heavily timbered.

Wilder than the first five wolves, they avoided human contact, and Callie knew it would be impossible to corral them and transfer them into the second kennel truck. They would have to ride the fire out, and she prayed they would survive. She had finally persuaded a reluctant Randy to leave the sanctuary while he could, before the access road became impassable. That had been almost three hours ago. Corralling her father into the truck was proving much more difficult than herding the wolves into the kennel cages.

Glancing over her shoulder, she saw the flames had drawn closer. The sound was tremendous, like a freight train roaring toward them, and the temperatures had soared to a scorching level. Her heart thudded hard against her ribs. She'd never known such terror. Not so much for herself, although she had no wish to burn alive, but for her father, whom she loved despite his failings. This was not how he was supposed to die.

But he had refused to leave.

Even now, when he was almost too weak to walk unaided, he resisted her, dragging his feet and straining toward the wolf enclosures. She hung on grimly to his arm, practically dragging him along, ignoring his protests. She only hoped he didn't have another heart attack. As frail as he was, he might not survive this time. But neither of them would survive if she didn't get them down the mountain.

Callie bore most of her father's weight as they stumbled across the front of his property, to where the kennel truck sat with the engine running in the small, gravel parking lot. Beneath the roar of the advancing flames, she could hear the low, plaintive moans of the wolves contained within the cages that were mounted on the back of the pickup.

Only five wolves.

Callie looked toward the enclosures beyond the outbuildings. There were ten separate pens surrounded by double-wire fencing and topped with concertina wire. She saw no sign of the remaining wolves.

"The pack." Her father wheezed, twisting toward the pens as he tried to break free of her grasp. "We have to bring them with us."

"We can't, Dad." They'd already gone over this a dozen times. "There's no more time. They have the bunkers. The only other option is to open the pens and release them."

Two years earlier, at Randy's urging, her father had installed underground, concrete bunkers in each enclosure for exactly this kind of scenario. Although they'd yet to be tested, the bunkers would provide some protection while the wolves were forced to shelter in place.

"I worry that the bunkers won't be enough," her father said, his voice breaking. "But if we release them, they could be killed."

Callie silently acknowledged the truth in what he said. The wolf was not a protected species in Montana. The best she could hope for was that the pack might cross into nearby Glacier National Park, where hunting was prohibited. But the more realistic scenario was that they would move in the other direction—away from the wildfire—and toward the towns of St. Mary and Browning. If that happened, they would almost certainly be shot on sight. While the sanctuary benefitted from the support of local businesses and volunteers, the ranchers in the region would not hesitate to protect their stock from a free-range wolf.

"We'll come back just soon as we can," she promised, putting an arm around him and steering him toward the pickup. "But we need to go, or we'll die."

"I can't leave them!" he cried. "We have to try one more time to evacuate them." With surprising strength, he broke free and lurched toward the pens, nearly falling in his haste.

With a cry of alarm, Callie ran after him, but he shoved her away. As thin as he was, she thought she might be able to carry him bodily to the vehicle, but hesitated when he turned blazing eyes on her.

"I won't leave them behind!" He was wild-eyed, and his color had gone nearly purple, which frightened her even more. He looked on the verge of having another heart attack.

She wanted to howl with frustration. Desperation lent her voice added strength. "Get your ass in the truck!" She'd never spoken to her father that way. "Now!"

Her heart fell when her father set his jaw in an expression she knew all too well.

"I'm not leaving my wolves behind." His hands clutched the fence, his fingers curling around the wire as he stared mutinously at her.

The heat had grown more intense. The roaring sound of the fire grew louder, more ominous. Soon, they would be trapped.

Callie swiftly considered her options. It would take her no more than a minute to retrieve the tranquilizer gun. One shot would be enough to knock her father unconscious, but the effects could kill him. They kept sedatives in the cabin, as well. She could load up a syringe and administer just enough to make him pliable, without losing consciousness. He'd fight her tooth and nail, otherwise. She hated the option, but she no longer had a choice.

Spinning on her heel, she sprinted toward the outbuilding that housed the office and the wildlife veterinary clinic. She was just feet from the door when movement from the far side of the property caught her attention. Flashes of yellow and red moved steadily through the trees. She paused, and as she watched, a small group of men emerged from the forest, hacking at the underbrush and branches with axes.

Firefighters!

She'd never seen anything as beautiful as the sight of those men in their yellow jackets and bright red hardhats, hefting axes and chainsaws and shovels as if they weighed no more than children's toys.

"Thank God," she breathed, and jogged toward them.

CHAPTER THREE

TYLER AND THE other two men quickly made their way along the length of wire fencing, and now Tyler could see a clearing ahead, and could just make out several buildings, and a pickup truck parked nearby. But the wildfire had moved fast. The tall pines behind the main house were fully engulfed. The air was thick with smoke and falling embers. He quickly radioed Sam that they had reached the property and would start the evacuation.

As they broke through the trees, Tyler took in the scene unfolding before them. A frail, elderly man stood clinging to the wire fencing of the wolf enclosure, while a young woman sprinted toward one of the outbuildings. As Tyler and his men broke through the trees, she skidded to a stop and stared at them with a mixture of astonishment and dawning comprehension.

As she approached them, the brightness of the flames silhouetted her, and Tyler had the strangest sense that time itself had slowed. The whole scene unfolded like something out of a Hollywood action movie, playing out in slow motion. He was acutely aware of everything, from the long strands of brown hair that blew across her face, to the way her jersey clung to her curves. He watched as her perfect mouth moved, aware she was shouting to them, but not hearing anything. Then, as if a switch had been thrown, everything rushed back into fast motion. Between the smoke, the ash, the heat of the fire itself, and the elderly man who still clung desperately to the fencing, he knew the scene could quickly turn deadly. Then there was the woman, who must be the daughter that Sam had spoken of. Not a child.

A beautiful woman.

And as he stepped forward to intercept her, she looked at him like he was some kind of superhero. Like he was her own personal knight in shining armor. Warning alarms blared in his head, and in that instant he realized there were some things more dangerous than either wolves or wildfire.

CALLIE CAME TO a stop in front of the first man, as the other two began cutting a fire line into the earth beyond the wolf enclosure.

"What the hell are you still doing here?" he shouted when he reached her side. His eyes traveled past her to the wall of flames that threatened to consume the house. "You need to leave! Now!"

"My father!" She turned and indicated where Frank stood by the wolf pen, glaring defiantly at them. "He won't go. He wants to stay with his wolves!"

The firefighter's eyes were red-rimmed and bloodshot

from the smoke, and now they narrowed as he took in the scene. Sweat ran down his face and created pale rivulets in the soot that smudged his skin. His gaze missed nothing and, after a brief second, he took Callie's arm and steered her toward the truck. "You need to haul ass down this mountain." His voice was rough, like sandpaper. "In another hour, the pass will be closed, if it's not already."

"But my father—"

"Give me a second."

She watched breathlessly as he jogged over to her father and bent his head to the older man. She couldn't hear their conversation, but after a moment her father nodded, and then leaned heavily on the firefighter's arm as they made their way to where Callie stood by the truck.

The firefighter helped her father into the cab, and then closed the door with a decisive slam. Rounding the hood of the truck, he pulled Callie slightly away from the vehicle.

"He doesn't look good." He had to shout to be heard about the roar of the flames. "He needs a doctor."

Callie's chest constricted in fear. "He had a heart attack just over a month ago," she confided. "He's only been home for a couple of weeks."

He spared a brief glance at the advancing flames before fixing his gaze on her. "Go straight to the hospital. Drive fast. Don't stop."

Callie nodded and reached for the door handle, but he forestalled her with one gloved hand over hers. She looked up at him, and her heart faltered again. She had no business noticing, but beneath the sweat and grime, he was compellingly attractive. Not handsome, exactly, but ruggedly male in a way that matched the rough quality of his voice. His eyes bored into hers.

"I mean it," he said, his voice low and grim. "You hit that pass, and you push that gas pedal to the floor. There's a road block at the base of the access road. I'll radio ahead to let them know you're coming, maybe they can have an ambulance waiting for you. They're keeping the road wet until you're safe. Don't stop until you're through, okay?"

Swallowing hard, she nodded. "Okay. What about you? Where's the rest of your crew?"

He grinned. The transformation to his face was so unexpected that for a moment Callie couldn't breathe. His teeth were startling white against the sooty darkness of his face, and deep grooves appeared in either lean cheek...not dimples, exactly, but something more extreme, and more powerful in their attraction. "This is what we're trained for. Don't worry about us."

Still Callie hesitated. "About the wolves...there are seven of them. Each pen has an underground bunker, and they'll probably hide out there. I doubt you'll even see them, but if you do, just let them be. They won't bother you or your men; they'll be too anxious to escape. Just...please don't hurt them."

The firefighter looked toward the flames, where the other

two men were busy clearing brush away from the advancing firestorm. His expression was somber. "If the wire fencing comes down and those wolves run, they'll head away from the wildfire, toward the towns. We'll keep the pens intact for as long as we can, but let's hope you're right and they stay in the bunkers."

"I'll come back," Callie promised. "If the pass is still open, I'll come back for them."

The man muttered something beneath his breath that sounded very much like a curse, and then he was hustling her into the truck. Before he closed her door, he leaned in. He was so close she could smell the ash and pine pitch that clung to him, see the tiny lines at the corners of his eyes, and the texture of his skin. A light stubble of beard growth shadowed his jaw, making his face even darker beneath the soot. His voice was a smoky rasp in her ear.

"Don't come back. The pass will be closed, and you won't make it through. Just get your father to a hospital. Drive fast. You'll make it."

He closed the door and thumped on the roof, before stepping back. With a last look at the wolf pens, Callie buckled herself in and accelerated out of the parking lot, churning up dirt and gravel. As she made her way down the long drive to the access road, she glanced in her rearview mirror. He still stood there, watching her, a lone black silhouette against the fiery backdrop. Then she rounded a bend, and he was gone.

BARRELING DOWN THE mountain road at breakneck speed was the most terrifying thing that Callie had ever done. She tried to focus on her driving, but thick smoke and ash billowed across the road, making visibility poor. Her hands were white-knuckled as they gripped the steering wheel. The truck hit a deep rut, and her father let out a small sound of distress as the vehicle pitched violently.

Glancing at him, Callie saw he was pale. A fine sheen of perspiration covered his face. He sat rigidly, his face contorted in a rictus of pain. Alarm flared through her.

"Dad! Are you okay?"

In response, he let out a soft groan and clutched his left arm. Callie dragged her attention back to the road, but her own heart thudded hard against her ribs.

Oh, God, please don't let him die!

They had nearly fifteen miles to go before they reached the closest town, and most of those miles were along the steep, rugged mountain pass. A towering ridge of pine trees hemmed the road in on one side, and a wall of rock and scrubby brush dominated the other side. Even if she dared to stop, she worried the dense growth would catch fire. If that happened, she and her father could very well become trapped.

The ash from the wildfire was falling thick enough that she was forced to use her windshield wipers, and now she leaned forward, peering intently through the sludge and grime accumulating on the glass. She could barely see the road. They reached a section where the ground fell away steeply on one side, with no guardrail or barrier. She prayed they didn't plunge off the mountainside, and tried to suppress the hysteria rising in her chest. Glancing at her father, she could see he was in distress, but she didn't dare to even slow down. The firefighter's last words kept repeating in her head.

Drive fast, don't stop.

"We're almost there, Dad," she said, hoping he didn't hear the way her voice wobbled on the lie. "Hang on."

As they rounded a bend, she saw with dismay that the ditches on either side of the road were burning, the flames spreading through the underbrush and licking at the edge of the hard-packed dirt road. Glancing upward through the windshield, she could see the trees to her left were fully engulfed in flames. Instinctively, she pressed the gas pedal harder. If one of those trees should come down across the road…

She didn't want to think about what might happen.

"Please, God," she whispered fervently, "just help me get safely to Browning, and I promise I'll never ask for anything else, ever again. I'll be a better daughter. I won't be such a bitch. I'll come back to Montana more often."

As if in answer to her prayers, the sky above them released a torrent of water, so abruptly and so heavy that it pounded the roof of the cab with a sound like thunder. Almost instantly, it was gone, and peering through the windshield, Callie saw a helicopter flying overhead, an empty water bucket swinging beneath it. Ahead of her, she could see the road was wet, and where there had been flames, now there was just steam and smoke. The helicopter had dumped the entire contents of the water bucket over both the truck and the road, at the precise moment when she needed it most.

In another ten minutes, they reached the main road that wound through the pass. The sky was ominously dark with smoke that her headlights did little to penetrate. Her father leaned heavily against his door. His eyes were closed and his breathing was labored. Callie frowned as she noted he still clutched his arm. Reaching over, she laid a hand on his shoulder.

"Dad, are you okay?"

He grimaced, but opened his eyes and looked at her.

His voice was little more than a rasp. "Drive faster."

Callie tried to control her rising panic. She didn't think they could travel any faster, at least not safely, but she was willing to try. She and her father had grown apart after she left home twelve years earlier to attend veterinary college in California, but that didn't mean she was willing to lose him. One of the reasons she'd come back to Montana after his heart attack was to try and salvage some kind of relationship with him before it was too late.

She refused to believe that it might be.

She pressed down on the gas pedal, trying to estimate

how much farther before they were through the pass. Negotiating the narrow mountain road frightened her on a good day, never mind when she was being pursued by a wildfire, with five wolves in the back of the truck, and a passenger who was suffering a heart attack. There was no doubt in her mind that her father was experiencing a major event; he was exhibiting all the classic signs.

"Hold on, Dad," she said, and grimly took the next curve faster than she would have dared at any other time. Over the course of the next several miles, she realized the smoke had dissipated and she could see blue skies and sunshine in the distance. Up ahead, she saw several emergency vehicles blocking the road, their red and blue strobe lights causing relief to surge through her. There, behind the fire and police vehicles, was an ambulance. Callie sent up a silent thank you to the firefighter for keeping his word.

She drew the pickup truck to the side of the road, the tires kicking up loose gravel as she braked. She jumped out as a uniformed sheriff's deputy approached. His expression was grim.

"Lady, do you have any idea how lucky you are to have gotten through the pass? The helicopter pilot radioed in that the road to the sanctuary is now fully engulfed by the wildfire. Another five minutes, and you wouldn't have made it." He ducked his head and peered past her to where her father sat clutching his arm. "Okay, let's get him into the ambulance."

"We wouldn't have made it if they hadn't dropped the water across the road," Callie confirmed. "There's a small fire crew at the wolf sanctuary right now, but that wildfire is right on top of them. There are only three of them; they'll be trapped or killed unless someone gets them out!"

"They're trained, and they have backup." The deputy nodded toward her father. "Let's focus on the immediate need."

Callie stepped back as two emergency medical technicians came around to her father's side of the truck and performed a quick evaluation of him. Then they helped him onto a gurney and loaded him into the ambulance.

"Will you ride with him?" the deputy asked.

She wanted to, more than anything. Her father looked gray and drawn as the medical team inserted an intravenous drip into his arm, and radioed ahead to the hospital. Her chest constricted, because she felt certain that this time, he wouldn't pull through. The strain of the past several hours had surely taken its toll, and this was her punishment for not insisting that they leave two days ago, before the situation became a crisis. For not being there when he needed her, not once during the past twelve years.

She felt sick.

"Are you okay?" The deputy wore an expression of concern. "Maybe you want to sit down and let someone take a look at you." He suggested. "You don't look too good."

Callie waved him off. "No, I'm fine. Really. Just get my

dad to the hospital."

They signaled for the ambulance to leave, and Callie watched with a sense of despair as the swirling red lights disappeared around a curve in the road. Passing a hand over her eyes, she turned back to her pickup truck. She'd follow the ambulance to the hospital, and then she'd figure out what to do with the wolves. Even now, their low keening caused the hair on her arms to rise.

"Where will you bring the animals?"

Callie shook her head. "I'm actually not sure. Randy, one of our assistants, is calling some of the other sanctuaries in the area to see if they can take them in, if only on a temporary basis."

"I hope that works out," the deputy said. "Nobody wants to see the wolves put down."

Callie looked at him sharply. That thought had never crossed her mind, and she would never allow that to happen to her father's wolves.

"Thanks for the support," she said drily. "I should get going."

The deputy stepped back as she climbed into the truck. He waved the blockade cars aside, before tipping his hat and signaling her through.

Callie blew out a hard breath. His words rankled. She hadn't risked life and limb to rescue the wolves, only to have them euthanized. The knowledge that the remaining seven wolves would likely perish in the wildfire was painful enough. She would find another home for the five she had in the truck, at least until they could return to the sanctuary.

If they could return.

Recalling the ferocity of the wildfire, and how close it had been to the house and the outbuildings, Callie knew there was little hope the structures would survive. She thought again of the firefighters.

Why had there only been three? Did they really have backup, as the deputy assured her?

She pictured the rugged man who had hustled her into the truck. She owed him her life. If he hadn't persuaded her father to get into truck when he did, they might not have made it through the pass. Hadn't the deputy said that if she'd been five minutes later, the road would have been impassable?

As she drove, she realized she was trembling. She had done it. Against the odds, she had made it through the pass. Her father was on his way to the hospital, where he would receive the care he needed. They had rescued five wolves. All in all, it was the best possible outcome, given the extreme circumstances. She just hoped the outcome for the three firefighters was as positive. She knew the likelihood of ever seeing the man again was slim to none. She didn't know his name, and had no idea which fire station he worked at. She made a mental note to stop by the fire marshal's office and inquire about the men who had tried to save the sanctuary, and had certainly saved her father's life.

She told herself she only wanted to thank him; her interest had nothing to do with a pair of shrewd eyes that missed nothing, or a grin that still made her knees go wobbly just thinking about it.

CHAPTER FOUR

C ALLIE NEGOTIATED THE long, winding descent that led to the small town of St. Mary. At this time of year, there were typically hordes of tourists in the region, eager to travel the famous Going to the Sun Road, which traversed Glacier National Park through some of the most stunning scenery in the world, and ended some fifty miles to the west, near the towns of Whitefish and Kalispell, Montana.

But the road had been partially closed for nearly two weeks as a result of the wildfires in the park, and Callie expected there were very few tourists lingering in either St. Mary or Browning, waiting for the closed portions to reopen.

As she emerged from the mountains into the flatlands, she saw dozens of emergency responders camped on a wide swath of meadow at the edge of St. Mary Lake. The entire field, which was part of larger campground, was covered with tents and trucks, and firefighting equipment. It seemed the scenic tourist spot had been turned into an incident command post.

As she drove past, she was a little taken aback by the sheer size of the operation. She'd been so occupied in caring for her father and helping with the wolves that she hadn't traveled to town in over a week. As a result, she'd completely missed just how large this wildfire was, and how many emergency personnel had been brought in to handle the crisis. If Randy hadn't risked his life by driving to their house that morning to alert them of the danger, they might not have escaped in time.

By the time she reached the hospital in Browning, she felt drained, both physically and emotionally. She parked the truck by the emergency entrance, and went inside to inquire about her father. An older nurse approached her, an expression of sympathy on her face.

"I've known your father for a long time," she said. "His heart's been giving him trouble for the past few years."

Callie nodded, wracked with guilt that it had taken her so long to visit. She should have come sooner. She would come more often, she promised herself. "Is he going to be okay?"

The nurse smiled reassuringly. "They're running tests on him now. We'll know more in a few hours." She clucked sympathetically and reached out to squeeze Callie's hand. "There's nothing you can do right now and worrying won't help. We'll take good care of him. What about you?"

Callie raised her eyebrows. "What about me?"

"Are you going to be okay?"

Her question gave Callie pause. She had five wolves outside in the kennel truck, and no place to safely house them.

Her father's ranch was likely nothing more than a pile of burnt cinders by now, which meant she had nowhere to go, either. Her thoughts turned to the three firefighters who were even now battling that monster blaze, and felt a renewed surge of guilt that she hadn't brought her father down from the mountain earlier. If she had paid closer attention to the news, or had left when the fire marshal had first come by, her father might not be suffering another heart attack. She would have had more time to move all the wolves to a safe location.

"I'll be fine." She assured the other woman, but inwardly she wasn't so sure. She'd never felt so overwhelmed or frightened in her entire life.

IN THE END, after hours of fruitless phone calls and visits to animal shelters, it became clear that there was no place in either St. Mary or Browning where Callie could safely leave the wolves. In fact, it seemed there wasn't anywhere on the eastern side of Glacier National Park where she could bring them.

She'd met Randy in the parking lot of the hospital, where he'd given her the discouraging news. He'd called every sanctuary he could think of, without success. Callie had hoped to find someone in the local area who might be willing to keep the pack while she attempted a return to her father's ranch. She spent several hours calling those friends of her father who owned ranches in the area, but none of them were willing to take the wolves.

Callie sat in cab of the pickup truck, wracking her brain for options. There must be someplace nearby where she could safely place the wolves. Not for the first time, she wished she hadn't stayed away from Montana for so long. There had been a time when she'd known everyone who lived in St. Mary, and she'd had friends in nearby Browning, as well. But when she graduated high school, she'd been anxious to leave and establish a new life for herself in California, where her mother lived.

On sudden impulse, she flipped through the contacts on her cell phone until she found Shayla Bullshoe's number. Shayla had been a childhood friend who had lived on the Blackfeet reservation, but she and her family had been frequent visitors to the wolf sanctuary. Eventually, Shayla had trained to become one of her father's veterinary assistants, helping with everything from feeding the wolves to performing routine checkups and minor surgeries, when required.

In the weeks since Callie had returned to Montana, she'd learned a lot about the sanctuary from Randy and Sarah, the two assistants. When Callie had asked about Shayla, she'd learned that she had stopped working at the sanctuary after the birth of her second child, claiming the drive was too long and, in the winter months, too treacherous. Now she worked at the local veterinary clinic, just outside of Browning. If the clinic couldn't take the wolves, Callie hoped Shayla might provide some recommendations on where else she might try.

When Callie pulled up to the clinic, she was taken aback by the tiny size of the facility, so unlike the sprawling animal hospital where she worked in Monterey, California. There, she was one of four veterinary physicians, and there was a support staff of more than a dozen people. They routinely saw sixty or more animals each day, mostly small pets, but Callie found the job fulfilling. Maybe it wasn't as exciting as raising wolves, but it paid her rent, and enabled her to be close to her mother, who lived in nearby Santa Cruz.

There were only three cars in the small parking lot, and when Callie pushed through the entrance door, the small waiting area was empty. A young woman sat behind a counter, and she looked up expectantly as Callie entered.

"I'm here to see Shayla, if she's in," Callie said, keeping one eye on the window, where she could see her pickup truck.

The girl's eyes widened slightly as they traveled over her, and Callie realized she looked as if she'd been battling the wildfire single-handedly. As the girl disappeared into the back of the clinic, Callie freed her long hair from the pony-tail holder and combed her fingers through the tangled strands, before securing it again. She swiped her hands over her shirt and jeans, trying to erase the worst of the dirt and soot. But there was no time to worry about her appearance, as the door swung open, and Shayla emerged.

With her glossy black hair and wide, dark eyes, Callie

would have recognized Shayla anywhere. Twelve years had changed her, adding fullness to her face and putting fine lines of experience at the corners of her eyes. She looked at Callie with a pleasant how-can-I-help-you expression on her face, before recognition hit her, and her eyes rounded with surprise.

"Callie!" Shayla pushed the swinging panel aside and came into the waiting area, arms extended.

Callie hugged the other woman briefly, before stepping back, smiling in spite of herself. "Shayla, it's so good to see you! How are you?"

Shayla grinned widely and put her hands on her swollen midriff. "Expecting baby number three in a few months. But enough about me! What is going on with you? I had no idea you were back in town."

The sight of Shayla's protruding belly caused something to hitch in Callie's chest. Something aching and bittersweet. She didn't need to examine the feeling to know what it was.

Yearning.

Maybe it was her own biological clock ticking, but lately Callie found herself thinking more and more about babies and family. She'd just turned thirty. Considering she didn't even have a boyfriend, she didn't hold out much hope that she'd have either anytime soon. While her work as a veterinary physician was both fulfilling and challenging, there were days when Callie thought she would cheerfully give it all up if she could just go home to needy, little arms that wanted hugs, and a pair of muscular arms that wanted to hold her. Instead, she had a dark, empty townhouse.

She'd been an only child. Her mother had left when Callie had been thirteen. She couldn't use the word *abandoned*, since Nancy McLain had invited Callie to spend several weeks each year in California with her, but at thirteen years old, it had sure felt like abandonment. And then there was her father...

The truth was, her father had abandoned her very early on, at least emotionally. His entire life centered around his wildlife sanctuary, and that didn't leave much room for an emotionally needy wife, or a young daughter.

Pushing the unpleasant memories aside, Callie hugged Shayla again. "I'm so, so happy for you," she said, meaning every word. "I can't wait to meet your other two children."

"I'll remind you that you said that." Shayla laughed. "They're a handful." She grimaced and reached out to swipe a thumb across Callie's cheek. She held it up to show her the blackened smudge. "What on earth have you been doing?"

Briefly, Callie explained what had happened at the ranch, glossing over the seriousness of her father's condition. Shayla had always admired Frank McClain, and Callie didn't want to upset her, not in her current state. Even so, Shayla's expression was one of shock and dismay.

"So dad's in the hospital undergoing some tests," Callie said quietly. "His house is likely gone, and I have two wolf packs in the back of the truck, and nowhere to bring them."

She gestured helplessly. "I was hoping you might have some ideas."

Shayla moved to one of the plastic chairs lined up against the wall, and sat down heavily. "I can't believe it. I brought the boys up there a just a few months ago. Everything seemed to be going so well for him."

Callie took the chair next to Shayla. "Yes, I think it was. He mentioned that he was finally turning enough of a profit to hire a third assistant. I think he recognized that he couldn't do as much as he used to, and was trying to step back into more of an administrative role, letting someone else handle the day-to-day care and feeding of the packs. But then he had a massive heart attack."

Reaching out, Shayla squeezed Callie's hand. "I'm so sorry. If only I'd known…"

"There was nothing you could have done." Callie assured her. "You have a family and a business to take care of. My father's been overdoing it for years, and he doesn't take care of himself. This was inevitable."

"But what about your own job? Your dad said you ran a vet clinic in California?"

Callie smiled. "I don't run the clinic. I work there with three other vets. They have someone covering for me while I take care of my dad. He was doing so well in his recovery that I actually thought I might go home next week. And now this…" She scrubbed her hands over her face. "I'll have to stay until we can find another place for my dad to live.

There's no way the house could have survived."

Callie's thoughts turned again to the men who had been fighting to keep the flames back from the ranch, and to the man who had helped her. Was he okay? Had he and his crew managed to wrestle control of the inferno, or had they put themselves in more danger by attempting to save the sanctuary? The images that rose to mind were horrifying in their clarity, and Callie had to push them aside. Just the thought of those brave men putting themselves in harm's way to save the ranch and the wolves made her feel ill.

"Most of the emergency responders arrived the day before yesterday," Shayla said, interrupting Callie's morbid thoughts. "I was shocked to see them. I'd no idea the wildfire had spread so far, or so quickly. The news reports made it sound as if the fire was under control, and that it wouldn't spread beyond the Lincoln Pass."

So Callie hadn't been the only one taken by surprise. "Yes, it was something of a shock to realize we were right in the path of the fire. We were warned two days ago that we might need to evacuate, but I didn't listen. One of my father's assistants, Randy, drove up to the sanctuary early this morning and helped us transfer some of the wolves to the kennel truck. Another assistant, Matt, tried to reach the sanctuary an hour later, and was turned back by the sheriff's men. He called us, and that's how we learned we were right in the path of the wildfire. Thank goodness Randy was able to leave when he did."

Shayla looked shocked. "I can't believe they didn't escort you out earlier."

Callie made a wry face. "They did try. My dad refused to leave. The only reason they didn't forcibly remove us was because the wildfire wasn't an imminent threat at that point, and I promised we would go the following day. They may not have realized we were still on the property."

"So what are you going to do now?"

"I don't know. I need to find a safe place for the wolves. I can't keep them in the truck indefinitely."

"There's a wolf sanctuary in Missoula."

"I called them. They said they can't take the pack, not on such short notice."

Shayla's eyebrows shot up. "Not even under these circumstances?"

Callie gave her a helpless look. "They already have three packs; they would need to construct more pens for our wolves, and that would take them a couple of days, even if they were willing to take them—which they're not."

"Hang on," Shayla said, pushing to her feet. "Let me make some phone calls. I may be out of the wolf business, but I still have some connections."

Smiling gratefully, Callie waited while Shayla went behind the counter and made a phone call. She spoke into the receiver, too low for Callie to hear. When she hung up several minutes later, her smile was triumphant.

"Missoula will take your pack, but only until you find a

permanent home for them."

Callie leapt to her feet. "Shayla, thank you! How did you do it? They would barely talk to me! They said they had no room for five wolves."

Her answering smile was sly. "I've always had a fascination with wolves, you know that. For a time, I dated the owner of the Missoula sanctuary, so I called in a favor. Besides, I know for a fact they have extra enclosures, in case they need to separate the wolves. In fact, don't be surprised if they agree to keep them permanently."

Callie laughed and hugged her friend. "Thank you, thank you."

Shayla pulled face as she stepped back. "There is a catch. They want you to pay for their upkeep while they're in Missoula."

"Of course, I'd expect nothing less." Relief flooded her. This was one less thing to worry about. "How soon can I bring them over?"

"Whenever you're ready. But there's another catch." Shayla actually looked embarrassed. "Call me shameless, but I could use your help here, if you have time."

Callie only barely concealed her surprise. The clinic was small, and it didn't look as if they were overrun with customers.

Seeing her expression, Shayla ran her hands over her burgeoning stomach. "My doctor said I need to rest more with this baby, but my assistant can't handle the work here on his own. He's capable, but he's not a physician." Her expression was pleading. "It doesn't seem as if you're going back to California anytime soon, and I could use an experienced vet to cover for me on the days that I can't make it in."

"Of course, just let me know what you need."

"I'll be here full-time through the end of the week, and will go part-time beginning next week. But we've also set up an animal rescue center over by the lake, for animals that have been burned or displaced by the fire, and that's where I could use your help. We have a dozen or so volunteers building shelters and feeding and caring for the animals, but we could use another vet for some of the more critical cases."

Callie nodded. "Absolutely. I'll head over there as soon as I can and check on the animals."

As she left the clinic, Callie pulled her phone out to contact Randy and let him know the good news. They could drive the wolves to Missoula that very day, and ensure they were settled into their new, albeit temporary, home. She just hoped everything else would be resolved as quickly.

CHAPTER FIVE

THE LINCOLN PASS wildfire was as vicious a fire as Tyler had ever seen. After the woman and her elderly father had left the property, he, Vin, and Ace had done what they could to protect the house and wolf enclosures, but the blaze had been too massive. The pens were constructed entirely of steel posts and wire, so there was a chance the fencing might withstand the intense heat of the wildfire. They'd called in for two water buckets to be dropped over the sanctuary, and then they had gotten the hell out of there. The house was a lost cause, and Tyler just hoped the wolves survived inside their concrete bunkers.

That had been almost four days ago.

Four days of battling one of the biggest fires he had ever seen. They'd rejoined the main group of smokejumpers on the southern edge of the fire, and had spent the last several days cutting fire lines and taking down rogue trees that had caught fire as the result of drifting embers. They'd been using coyote tactics, a progressive line construction duty that entailed building fire lines until the end of the day, and then bedding down wherever they ended up, without the benefit of even a sleeping bag.

Tyler figured he'd had about six hours of sleep in the last four days, snatched when the winds had died down during the night. They'd set up a field camp a little farther to the south, and the base had dropped in some additional supplies, since each firefighter only carried enough food and water to last for a couple of days.

Now they were positioned about a quarter of a mile ahead of the main fire, digging lines and removing as much flammable material as they could. They were working on a slope, and Tyler could hear the crackle of the flames as the front moved closer. His back and shoulders ached from swinging the pickaxe, and it was only his training and commitment to his crew that kept him going.

As he worked alongside Vin, methodically clearing the undergrowth, he thought again about the wolf sanctuary, and the woman he'd encountered there. He still couldn't believe she and her father had waited so long to leave. The nightmarish scene kept playing over in his head. The flames had literally been at the back door and yet there they were, dicking around instead of hightailing it out of there.

What the hell had the woman been thinking?

Why she hadn't moved her father and the wolves down the mountain days earlier?

He loved his job, but these were the kinds of situations that made him crazy. He'd take on a wildfire any day over a stubborn woman. At least he'd been able to talk sense into the old man, telling him his daughter would die if he didn't get her down the mountain. The warning seemed to give the old guy a start, as if he hadn't once considered the danger to his daughter.

After the girl and her father left the sanctuary, Tyler had radioed ahead for an ambulance to meet them at the bottom of the pass. He'd waited another thirty minutes before he'd contacted the emergency personnel who were manning the pass. They confirmed the kennel truck had arrived safely, but only with the help of an aerial water dump.

After reassuring himself that the woman and her father were safe, he'd called in for a second water dump over the sanctuary, in an attempt to protect the pens. Beyond that, there hadn't been anything more they could do for the wolves, and he hoped they had retreated underground, to the bunkers. Once the wildfire was under control and the area around the sanctuary was safe, he intended to go back and check on the wolves himself. With luck, he could do that the following day. He didn't hold out much hope for their survival, but there was always a chance.

"Hey, boss," he called over to Sam, who was digging a hell of a trench. "Any chance I can take some guys and check on that property we evacuated?"

"There's nothing left, I guarantee it," Sam replied.

"Still, I'd like to check on those animals, see if they made it."

Sam stopped digging and leaned on his pulaski, looking

exasperated. "And what? They're wolves, Dodson, not lapdogs. Even if they did survive—which is unlikely—what could you do? You're not going to be able to throw a leash on them and walk them out."

"Is that a yes?" Tyler gave him a level look. "We're only a couple of miles from the site. I figure the fire has already passed over the area, and we can at least go in and do some mop-up."

Sam removed his hard hat and used his arm to wipe the sweat and grime from his face. "Let's see how far we get cutting this line, first. If we can get this bitch under control, then we can talk mop-up."

Tyler returned to swinging his pickaxe, feeling a little better. Even if they discovered the worst, at least he would know.

Overhead, a helicopter carrying an enormous bucket of water from nearby St. Mary Lake, dumped the contents over the leading edge of the wildfire, sending thousands of gallons of water into the conflagration and causing a cloud of steam to hiss through the air. Heat rolled over Tyler. His exposed skin felt tight, and even with the protective goggles, his eyes were fried. Despite drinking gallons of water, his body felt as if all the moisture had been sucked out of it. More than that, the air pressure was changing as the monstrous wildfire consumed the available oxygen.

They needed to retreat. Tyler had been fighting wildland fires since he was old enough to carry a pulaski, and there wasn't anything he'd rather do for a living. He'd battled blazes throughout the country, including Alaska, and Canada, but nothing propelled him into action faster than when a wildfire that threatened his own home state.

He'd grown up exploring the park's interior, hiking the mountain peaks, and swimming in the cold, pristine lakes. Logically, he understood wildfires happened and they weren't always a bad thing. But this one was like a ferocious dragon, consuming everything in its path and leaving nothing but a wake of destruction and charred earth behind. The dry conditions, fueled by strong winds and warm temperatures, were a recipe for disaster. The fire seemed to have a mind of its own, shifting directions and leaping across fire lines at will.

The crew had been working line construction for several hours now, and for the entire day the winds had worked to their advantage, blowing the fire back onto itself. The aerial crews had been dumping water onto the flames as fast as they could scoop it out of the nearby lake, but the heat was so incredibly intense that even the massive dousing wasn't enough to completely suppress the flames.

They'd made some good progress, but Tyler knew the precise moment when the wind changed, reversed direction, and began blowing ash and embers down the slope, directly on top of their position. The entire crew watched in silent horror as a fiery trail of hot cinders drifted over their heads and landed in the dry grasses below them, bursting into flames wherever they touched down.

"Jesus Christ." Sam breathed beside him, and then yanked out his radio. "Crew 1-Glacier Creek to base, come in!" There was no reply. He tried again, "Crew 1-Glacier Creek to base! Do you copy? Answer, goddamn it!"

Tyler could see the danger. There was no way they could extinguish the dozens of grass fires popping up all over the slope, but if they didn't move, they'd be trapped between two walls of flame. It didn't matter now which way the wind blew, they were screwed.

Sam was hollering down the line for the men to haul ass to the west, beyond the line of burning trees to where the most recent water drop had soaked the forest. If they could get beyond the trees that were fully engulfed, before the grass fires closed off that route, they might have a chance. But it was more than a hundred yards, uphill, and they'd been busting their asses for more than twenty-four hours.

They began running.

Tyler had been working the end of the construction line, and consequently found himself at the back of the retreating men. He hung onto his pulaski and forced his legs to move, his breath coming in hard pants as he sprinted hard, keeping one eye on the trees, and watching as fireballs shot over their heads. Ahead of him, someone tripped and went down, and Tyler reacted instinctively, grabbing the man's jacket and hauling him back to his feet, and then pushing him ahead. The air wavered with the intensity of the heat, and Tyler's head was filled with the roaring of the flames that raced toward them.

Grassfire was the fastest kind of wildfire. No man could outrun it, and Tyler could see their escape route was rapidly closing. In another ten seconds, they'd be running through the fire itself. He could almost feel the flames licking at his feet. In all the years he'd been fighting fires, he'd never had to deploy his fire shelter, but sensed that was about to change.

Sam had stopped running, and was shouting into his radio while simultaneously waving the men past him, and directing them toward a section of trees that still gave off damp steam from the recent water drop. The men at the front of the line had just reached the tree line, but there was no way the guys at the back would make it before the fire trapped them.

As the crew foreman, Tyler was getting ready to give the order to deploy the fire shelters, when he heard the unmistakable drone of a low-flying airplane overhead. He didn't even look up, but instead took a knee and covered his face, just seconds before the slurry hit him.

The impact might have driven him to his knees if he wasn't already down. As he felt the thick, cold gel coat his body and begin to slide beneath the edge of his jacket, he lifted his head. The plane had made a direct hit, covering both the men and the meadow with the fire retardant, effectively dousing the fire and saving their lives.

A whoop went up from the men, and Tyler pushed himself to his feet, swiping the emollient from his shoulders and arms. The once flaming grass was now nothing more than a blackened, smoking wasteland. As Tyler made his way toward the other men, a second helicopter made a pass over the still-burning trees, and emptied the bucket over the canopy, preventing additional embers from escaping.

"Okay, boys," Sam called, "we're not done here yet! Shake it off, and let's finish this."

Tyler bent forward, bracing his hands on his knees as he sucked in deep breaths. The air was filled with ash, and the heat was still incredible, but it was nowhere near what it had been just scant seconds ago. If not for the two aerial drops, he'd likely be nothing more than a charred lump. He still couldn't comprehend how quickly the situation had changed, when they thought they'd had control, and then it was gone. In all his years of battling wildfires, this was the closest he'd ever come to thinking he might not make it home.

Hefting his pickaxe, he turned back to the line of trees and began working the fire line once again. He threw himself into the work, glad for the distraction. Later, he would have time to go over what had just happened. He'd never been a man to waste time over regrets, but he suddenly regretted that aside from his mother, there wasn't anyone who would miss him if he didn't return from a call.

He thought again of the pretty girl at the sanctuary. His

passing would have no more impact on her life than that of a passing breeze. With that sobering thought, he bent to his work, deciding it might be time to make some changes in his life.

CALLIE BENT TO inspect the wound more closely, making soothing noises that did little to calm the frightened dog that lay squirming on the makeshift examination table. She'd spent most of the last several days at the animal rescue center that had been hastily set up near St. Mary Lake. Local volunteers had erected two large tents, and had built several wire enclosures for the larger animals that were coming in. Smaller animals were kept in crates under the first tent, while three plywood tables served as crude examination and operating tables.

Already, they had quite an assortment of animals, from cats and dogs to deer, and even a badger. Not all of the animals were injured. Some of them were merely displaced as a result of the fire, and the rescue center became their temporary home. Volunteers were kept busy looking for foster homes in the area, but Callie could see it wouldn't be long before they would need additional crates and enclosures.

"Hold him still, please." She instructed the two women who assisted her.

The dog, a large mixed-breed, had been found wandering, dazed and limping, along the stretch of road that led into town. He had no collar, and as far as Callie could tell, no identifying tattoo or microchip with which to trace him. He'd been burned, and the fur on his face, chest, legs, and tail had been scorched completely off. From what she could see, most of his burns were superficial, but there was a wound on his leg that concerned her.

"This guy was in some sort of a fight." She gently probed the injury. "It looks like a bite, and it's become badly infected." She glanced up. "Hand me that saline, would you, Kim?"

One of the women handed her a squirt bottle, and Callie flushed the wound. "Okay, I'll need to stitch this, but let's make him a little more comfortable first."

Selecting several vials from her medical kit, she prepared an injection to help with the pain, and administered it deftly, before giving the dog several shots of local anesthetic around the bite wound. When he finally relaxed under the effects of the sedative, she cleaned the wound and then closed it with a dozen stitches, before wrapping the leg with gauze. When that was done, she liberally applied a soothing gel to the burned areas of his face and body, wrapping those as well, until he looked more like a mummy than a dog.

"He's badly dehydrated," she said, lifting the dog's lip to examine his gums. "Let's get a fluid line into him, and start him on antibiotics."

Together, the three women lifted the sheet under the dog, and carried him into one of the wire enclosures nearby, setting him carefully down on the blankets. Callie inserted the IV drip, and satisfied that he was resting comfortably, closed the pen and stepped back.

"When he comes around, offer him some water, but just a little at a time," Callie said. "Keep the fluids going for the next six hours, and keep him quiet. Drape a blanket over the top of the pen to keep the sun off him, and I'll check on him in a couple of hours."

She glanced at her watch. It was past noon. She'd been at the rescue site for nearly four hours, and had taken care of the worst of the injured animals. There were six volunteers, and they'd set up a rotating schedule so that there were always three people on duty. One of the older volunteers had some veterinary experience, although she'd been retired for almost ten years, but Callie knew the animals were in good hands. She needed to see her father. He'd been heavily sedated when she'd visited him earlier, which was almost a relief.

Since escaping the fire, Callie hadn't been able to return to the sanctuary to check on the wolves, and consequently she had no idea if they had survived. So far, she'd been able to avoid answering his questions about the wolves, but she knew that would be the first thing he would ask about, and she dreaded not having an answer for him.

Randy had driven the five wolves to Missoula, and had returned the day before with the empty kennel truck. Callie was relieved to know the five wolves were safely settled into their new home. Climbing into the truck, she made the drive from St. Mary to Browning. The road took her past the emergency command post, where the firefighters and rescue personnel had set up their camps. There were units from all over the state of Montana, and even from other states. They had spread out along the shore of the lake, occupying a field that was normally a campground for tourists. Peering through her windshield, Callie could see the dull haze of smoke in the distance, spreading out over the mountains.

On impulse, she pulled her truck into the field, and parked next to a St. Mary rescue vehicle. She sat for a moment, considering. Was she crazy to make inquiries about the men who had tried to save her father's property? She had no idea which unit they were from, and there were literally dozens of units encamped by the lake, with more than three hundred men involved in the fire suppression. There was no way she'd be able to find three men—okay, one man, if she was being honest with herself. And what would she say, anyway?

With a self-deprecating groan, she started the truck and was about to reverse out of the field, when she saw the St. Mary Fire Chief walking with two other men, their heads bent over a map. Before she could change her mind, Callie climbed out of the truck and hurried across the field to intercept them.

"Chief Olsen, do you have a minute?"

The men stopped, and after a quick word with his companions, the fire chief approached Callie. "Can I help you?"

"Yes, I'm Frank McLain's daughter, Callie. He operates the wildlife sanctuary off the access road."

The fire chief nodded. "I know Frank. I'm sorry to hear about your troubles. What can I help you with?"

Chief Olsen was a mountain of a man, with a deep, barrel chest and enormous shoulders. His weathered face was as hard and unyielding as the rest of him. Callie suddenly wished she hadn't bothered him.

"Well…" She clasped her hands together and gave him an earnest smile. "I was hoping you might have some news about my father's property. We were forced to leave some wolves behind, and since I haven't been able to return, I thought maybe one of your men had some news?"

"No, I'm sorry. I understand they sent resources in to remove both you and your father, but those men were unable to stay and protect the property. Unfortunately, the fire was just too large."

"Actually, I was hoping you might have the names of the men who helped us." She gestured awkwardly. "So that I can thank them."

Chief Olsen shook his head. "No, I don't have their names."

Disappointment swamped Callie.

"But you can check with the Glacier Creek base," he continued. "They were part of the smokejumper crew stationed out of Glacier Creek. Is there anything else?"

Callie beamed at him. "No! Thank you, you've been very

helpful."

She could hardly keep the lightness out of her step as she returned to her truck.

Smokejumpers.

Somehow, the knowledge didn't surprise her. She had already been impressed by their fearlessness in battling the wildfire, but the knowledge that they were smokejumpers only increased her respect and admiration for them. She didn't know much about firefighting, but she knew smoke-jumpers and hotshots were the elite; the special forces of the wildland firefighting community. The last line of defense between an out of control wildfire and those it threatened. It was enough to give her the shivers, even on a hot summer day like today.

Glacier Creek was located on the other side of Glacier National Park, north of Missoula. She estimated it would take about six hours to drive there from St. Mary, taking the longer route around the park, since the road through the park was closed. She made a promise to herself that when she went out to Missoula in a few days to check on the wolves, she would visit the Glacier Creek base and extend her personal thanks to the men who risked their lives to help her. The smokejumpers would likely still be battling the wildfire, but she would leave something for them to demonstrate her gratitude and appreciation.

On that thought, she pulled into the parking lot of the small hospital, and made her way toward the cardiac wing.

The air conditioned interior was a welcome relief from the outside heat. As she walked through the outpatient wing, Callie lifted her long hair away from her neck and wound it into a loose knot at the back of her head, securing it with an elastic band. As she passed one of the outpatient rooms, she had a swift glimpse of a man lying on the bed with an oxygen mask over his mouth and nose. A nurse stood on one side of the bed, administering an IV. Callie took several steps beyond the door when she stopped abruptly, struck by recognition.

No, it couldn't be. Could it?

Slowly, she retraced her steps and peered around the doorframe just enough to see inside the room. He lay back against the pillows, his face still smudged with soot, and an IV hooked to one arm. Without a doubt, it was her firefighter.

He wore a hospital gown, but his heavy work boots stood guard at the base of his bed, and a red hard hat sat on a nearby chair. His eyes were closed, and he didn't look quite as hard or tough as she remembered. As the nurse checked his vitals, she said something too low for Callie to hear. The man didn't respond, but beneath the clear plastic mask, his mouth curved upward in a wry smile, and there was no mistaking the telltale dents in his cheeks.

And all Callie could think was, *I've found him.*

CHAPTER SIX

S LOWLY, CALLIE STEPPED into the room and approached the bed. The nurse smiled at her and continued to adjust the IV tubing. Callie looked down at him for a long moment. Without his hard hat, she could see his hair was dark brown, with lighter streaks of gold. His jaw was shadowed with even more stubble than before. Traces of dirt and soot coated his face and the strong column of his throat.

As if sensing her scrutiny, he opened his eyes and looked directly at her. Callie felt her breath catch. His irises were a shade of pure blue-green, as clear as a mountain lake. Why hadn't she noticed that earlier? His eyes were still red-rimmed and bloodshot, but there was no mistaking the sudden recognition that flared in their depths. Immediately, he shoved himself into a sitting position, and yanked the oxygen mask from his face.

"Hey."

"It's you."

They spoke at the same time, and Callie broke off with an embarrassed laugh, feeling warm color spread up her neck.

"I'm sorry," she said. "I didn't mean to disturb you. It's just that I was walking past, and I thought I recognized you."

"No, it's fine," he said. His voice was hoarse and raspy, as if he'd inhaled smoke. His eyes never left hers. "Pull up a chair."

Glancing around, Callie carefully moved his helmet to the bedside table and drew the chair close to the bed. She was acutely aware of his eyes traveling over her and missing nothing. She knew she looked a wreck, but she was willing to bet she didn't look nearly as bad as he did. "You should put your oxygen back on."

"Yes, you should." The nurse affirmed and, ignoring his protests, retrieved the mask and settled it over his face, only to have him pull it down beneath his chin so that he could continue talking.

"What happened to you?" Callie asked. "Are you hurt?"

"No, it's nothing, I'm fine." He assured her, shooting a warning glance at the nurse.

"He's suffering from smoke inhalation, heat exhaustion, and severe dehydration," the nurse contradicted him. She gave Tyler a hard look. "He needs rest, plenty of fluids and oxygen, but he should be fine in a *day or two.*"

Callie didn't miss how she placed added emphasis on the last three words, letting him know in no uncertain terms he wasn't going anywhere, at least not today. Callie could see he wanted to argue the point, but instead he clamped his mouth shut and shrugged, as if he actually had a choice in the matter and was simply letting the nurse have her way.

The nurse gave him an indulgent smile. "I'll let you visit for a bit, but you need to keep your oxygen on."

"Yes, ma'am." He made no move to replace the mask.

The nurse left, and there was a brief, awkward silence.

"How's your father?"

"Thank you for saving my father."

They spoke at the same time again, and Callie laughed again, covering her face. "Sorry. How about I go first?"

He spread one hand. "Please."

"Okay." She extended a hand toward him. "I'm Callie McLain."

She found her hand clasped warmly in his bigger one, feeling the hard calluses on his palm. "Nice to meet you, Callie. I'm Tyler Dodson."

Callie withdrew her hand, reluctantly. "I was hoping to see you again; I wanted to thank you for what you did the other day, helping me get my dad out of there. He wasn't cooperating, and if you hadn't shown up when you did, I'm not sure what I would have done." She rolled her eyes. "Well, I know what I was about to do, but it wouldn't have been pretty."

At his questioning look, she made a face. "I was either going to shoot him with a tranq gun, or give him a shot of a sedative that's usually reserved for the wolves."

Tyler gave a bark of laughter, and then winced.

"Are you okay?" Callie asked.

"Yeah, just a little scorched lung; nothing to worry about."

Callie frowned. "Did they do any chest x-rays? Have they ruled out pulmonary edema?"

Tyler's eyes narrowed. "Yes, and yes. What are you, a doctor?"

"I'm a veterinary physician, but I've treated my share of animals for smoke inhalation." She paused. "Not that you're an animal."

This time there was no mistaking his wry grin. "Some might disagree."

"How did it happen? Not trying to save my father's property, I hope!"

He hesitated. "We were working a fire line on a steep slope, and a secondary blaze sprang up behind us. We started running ahead of it, and got an aerial assist with a slurry dump, but the entire area was filled with ash and particulate matter. It happened fast; none of us were wearing our masks, and I guess I just inhaled more than my share."

He was getting tired, she could see that. Pushing her chair back, she stood up. "I should let you rest. Did they say when you might be released?"

"I decide that," he responded, and Callie almost smiled.

She wondered if he realized how serious smoke inhalation could be. Sometimes, symptoms didn't manifest until several days after the event.

"Well, it can't hurt for you to stay here for today, at

least," she said. "I'll check in on you before I leave. Can I bring you anything?"

"I can't think of anything."

"Okay, then." She gave him a bright smile. "I guess I'll be going, then. Get some rest."

She turned to leave, but he reached out and caught her wrist, stopping her.

"There is one thing."

Callie waited, aware that his fingers around her wrist were doing odd things to her heart rate.

"What?" Her voice sounded breathless.

"We did go back to the sanctuary. I'm sorry, but your house is gone."

"And the wolves?" Callie held her breath.

"The wire fencing was still intact. We counted five wolves that survived, not sure about the other two. We found the meat locker, and threw them some food. They were pretty hungry."

Callie's heart leapt. Five wolves were alive! And if he and his crew were able to return to the sanctuary, then maybe she could get back there, too. It was the best possible news. On impulse, she leaned down and kissed him. It was meant for his cheek, as a gesture of thanks and gratitude, but he turned his face and her lips found his mouth, instead.

For a moment, she was too surprised to pull away. Then his mouth began to move beneath hers and she no longer wanted to. His lips were warm and surprisingly gentle, fusing with hers in a kiss so sweet Callie's toes curled.

"Goddamn it, Dodson, I leave you alone for ten minutes, and you go all code blue on me."

At the sound of the masculine voice, Callie jerked away, breaking the kiss, and taking two unsteady steps away from the bed.

A big, good-looking firefighter lounged against the doorframe, a Styrofoam cup of coffee in one hand and a knowing smirk on his face. "I mean, that *was* a lifesaving resuscitation effort I just witnessed, right? Because if it was something else, just say the word and I'll leave. I'll even close the door and give you both some privacy."

Callie could feel a hot wash of color spread to the roots of her hair. "It's okay, I was just leaving."

She glanced at Tyler, who was holding the oxygen cap over his face and drawing on it as if he'd just run a marathon. She didn't know whether to be insulted or flattered.

"I'll see you later."

The big guy in the doorway stepped aside to let her pass. "Don't let me interrupt," he said, grinning.

"You weren't; I has just on my way out," she said, and fled.

But as she walked quickly away, she heard him say, "Christ, if that's the kind of bedside service they're providing these days, sign me up."

Callie couldn't prevent a smile. As bedside service went, she knew she could *do* better. Much better.

ACE PULLED UP the chair Callie had recently vacated, a knowing gleam in his eye. "Tell me that wasn't the chick from the wolf sanctuary."

"Okay," Tyler agreed, "I won't."

Now that she was gone, he could relax. He'd never felt so exposed as he did sitting there, wearing a damned johnnie, with a plastic oxygen cap over his face. Now he breathed deeply, feeling the tightness in his chest begin to ease. As Ace began relating what he'd missed at the base camp that morning, Tyler slid back down in the bed and settled himself more comfortably against the pillows.

He hadn't known he was close to collapse following the backfire, only that he'd sucked in his share of smoke and ash. After containing the wildfire, Sam had kept half the crew back to do mop-up, and had directed Tyler and a smaller group to hike back to the sanctuary to see if anything could be salvaged, and do any required mop-up there, as well.

The sanctuary had looked just about as bad as Tyler had expected. The house had been nothing but a pile of charred timbers surrounding the fireplace, which was still standing. The concrete outbuilding had been intact, although the metal roof had warped from the intensity of the heat and the windows had blown out. Inside, everything was a ruin except for the walk-in cooler, which was virtually unscathed.

Tyler and the others had pulled out buckets of meat and tossed them into the wolf enclosures which, remarkably, were still standing. Inside the pens, the land was nothing more than blackened earth with some ghostly charred trees. But then something amazing had happened. When they'd chucked the meat into the pens, the wolves had begun to show themselves, furtive shadows that quickly darted out to grab the food and drag it away to eat.

They'd left some water out for the animals, and then scoured the property, looking for any hot spots and performing mop-up. They'd just finished, and had been heading back to the base camp when he'd found himself struggling to breathe. Really struggling. He'd barely managed to alert Vin before he'd blacked out. Stupid, really, because all the warning signs had been there. He'd just ignored them, which was exactly what he warned the newbies not to do. For a guy who was all about safety, he didn't set much of an example.

Ace was still talking about the backfire and how they'd almost had their asses fried, but Tyler found he was no longer paying attention. Settling back, he closed his eyes and let his thoughts drift to Callie.

To that kiss.

That was why he loved his job. Because sometimes, between the bone-crushing, achingly long days of wielding a pickaxe or chainsaw in the very teeth of hell, covered in sweat and grime, feeling as if his lungs had been charred and his eyeballs roasted, he might get a kiss from a pretty woman.

And she was damned pretty.

When he'd opened his eyes to see her bending over him, he'd wondered if he was dreaming. When he'd first seen her at the sanctuary, he'd had an almost visceral response to her. He'd tried to convince himself that his immediate and powerful reaction to her had been the result of adrenaline, and the urgency of their situation. But he knew he was lying to himself. His entire world had stopped for an instant, and when it had swung back into motion, everything had changed. He'd realized she was attractive, but seeing her up close, that word didn't come close to describing Callie McLain.

She was drop-dead gorgeous and sexy as all hell.

He'd wanted to lose himself in the deep chocolate of her eyes, bury his hands in the gleaming waves of her dark hair. Her skin was smooth and creamy, except for a small beauty mark at the corner of her right eye. And then she'd kissed him with her soft, pink mouth.

Not that there weren't plenty of women who wouldn't be happy to kiss him. On any Friday or Saturday night, The Drop Zone pub was filled with women who went there with the single intention of going home with a firefighter. The guys at the base called them fireflies, or in the case of the smokejumping crew, jumper-humpers. Tyler had even gone home with one or two of them himself, right after Alicia had left him and he was feeling bitter and sorry for himself. But it had been over a year since he'd had a one-night stand. He wasn't averse to hooking up once in a while, as long as the woman understood that it was just sex.

He'd had a couple of relationships, but neither had lasted

more than a few months, and even those had been more casual than serious. He told himself it was for the best, since most women wanted marriage, and he'd decided long ago he wasn't ever going to do that again. Not even if his mother *had* recently hinted that she'd like some grandchildren. No way was he taking the bait. Tyler had seen what marriage to a smokejumper had done to his mother, and even if she never complained, he knew there had been weeks when she lived alone, unable to sleep, wondering if Mike would come safely home. Tyler wouldn't put any woman through that.

His only interest was to get healthy enough to return to his crew and work the fire. But if pretty Callie McClain wanted to keep him company until that time, he had no argument. But once the wildfire was suppressed, any sparks between himself and Callie would be extinguished, as well. He couldn't see any reason to start anything with her that he had no intention of continuing with.

"Hey, you listening to me, or pretending to sleep?" Ace asked, interrupting his thoughts. In response, Tyler gave an exaggerated snore, which sent him into a paroxysm of coughing. Ace handed him a cup of water. "So what's the story with you and the wolf-girl?"

Pulling the mask aside, Tyler cracked an eyelid and gave him a warning look. "There is no story. She's a nice lady who just wanted to say thank you."

Ace slanted him a sly smile. "That was a hell of a thank you."

"Stop talking, Ace."

Ace laughed. "Oh, man, you are in serious trouble, my friend." Tyler didn't open his eyes; didn't want to give the other man any reason to rib him further. But he knew Ace was right—he was in trouble.

CHAPTER SEVEN

CALLIE SPENT SEVERAL hours sitting at her father's bedside, although she doubted he would remember. He had been moved out of the intensive care unit and into a regular room, but he was still weak and heavily medicated. He would need to spend at least another week or two in the hospital, and would then go to a rehab facility before they could send him home.

Home.

Callie hadn't yet told her father that he no longer had a home to return to. He was so frail she feared the news might finish him. Instead, she'd told him his wolves had survived, and the firefighters had returned and provided them with food and water. He'd wept at the news, but had grown quiet when she went on to say she'd found a second sanctuary willing to take the surviving wolves, but it was in Wyoming. Callie understood the relief he must feel at knowing his wolves were safe, but when he'd begun talking about repairing the enclosures, and bringing all the wolves back, she hadn't been able to listen. She'd kissed him, told him to rest, and had left him alone.

Realistically, she knew she'd have to break the news about the property to him, but wanted to wait until he was stronger. In some respects, the wildfire had been a blessing in disguise. With his home destroyed, her father would have no reason not to return to Monterey with her.

She'd peeked in at Tyler on her way out, but his eyes had been closed, so she hadn't stopped. Even if he had been awake, she wasn't certain she would have gone in. She wouldn't have been very good company.

For as long as she could recall, her father had operated the wildlife sanctuary. She'd helped him out as a teenager not just because she'd enjoyed the work, but because she had hoped it would bring them closer, especially after her mother had left. But Frank, himself a veterinarian, hadn't seemed to appreciate her efforts to impress him. She might have been just another volunteer for all the notice he took of her.

Even now, he didn't seem to understand how much she was doing for him, taking time off from her own job, away from her home and friends, to ensure he was taken care of. He would have been in a rehab facility long ago if she hadn't agreed to come out from California and take care of him. She wasn't looking for accolades, just some acknowledgment. But some people didn't change, and that was a reality she was finally beginning to face. Her mother had once tried to explain to her that while her father did love her, he wasn't capable of demonstrating that, either verbally or through actions. He was emotionally limited, and Callie need to accept that he couldn't give her what she wanted. As a doctor, Callie understood this. But as a daughter, she couldn't help but wish things were different.

She and Randy had spent most of the night making calls to other wolf sanctuaries around the country, and Callie had been elated when a wolf rescue center in Wyoming had agreed to take the surviving wolves on a permanent basis. Once they were able to return to the sanctuary and rescue the remaining wolves, Randy would make the long, fourteen hour drive to Cheyenne, and help get the wolves settled.

She pulled the kennel truck into the campground where the fire fighting units had made their base camp near the lake. The animal rescue location was on the far side of the complex, and the town managers had arranged for Callie to stay in one of the small campground cabins while she worked with the rescued animals. For now, it was perfect for her needs, with a small living area and kitchenette, a bedroom, and a bathroom.

Callie parked the truck and climbed out, surveying the activity where the firefighters and rescue crews had set up their quarters. Pushing her hands into the pockets of her jeans, she worked her way between the tents, trailers, and trucks, stepping over enormous power cords and around generators. Firefighters were sacked out on the ground, catching some sleep beneath the shade of several canopies, while others sat in camp chairs in small circles, or stood grouped around folding tables, examining maps. Several looked up and nodded to her as she made her way past.

"Excuse me," she said, stopping outside a tent hung with a banner that read *Glacier Creek Smokejumpers.*

Beneath the canopy, three men were studying a map that had been tacked to a large board, talking in low tones. Callie could see it was a topographical map of the region, and there were a dozen or more small flag pins in varying colors stuck into the map.

The men turned to look at her, their expressions a combination of polite inquiry. "Can I help you," asked the first man.

"Yes, my name is Callie McLain. I just came from the hospital where I visited with Tyler Dodson. I understand he's with your group?"

She didn't miss the glances that passed between the men. As the first man stepped forward, the two other men bent their heads together, and Callie was certain she heard the words *wolf-girl* in their hushed exchanged. She suppressed a smile. They had no way of knowing that her nickname in high school had been wolf-girl, and sometimes *she-wolf* if she was having a bad day.

"I'm Captain Sam Gaskill." The first man extended his hand to Callie. "Tyler is one of our best. How do you know each other?"

Callie was pretty sure the captain already knew how she and Tyler were acquainted, especially if his men were referring to her as wolf-girl.

"My father owns the wolf sanctuary up off the fire road," she explained. "Tyler told me that he and some of the others went back there this morning to check on the wolves that we had to leave behind."

Sam nodded. "That's right." He paused. "I'm very sorry about your house, ma'am. There wasn't anything left when we returned. But we're confident at least five of the wolves did survive the blaze, and we made sure they had enough food and water to last another day or so."

"Thank you," Callie said. "I'm so grateful to you and your men for everything you've done. I was wondering…is there any chance I can return to the sanctuary to extract the remaining wolves? With their habitat destroyed, and the main house gone, they can't stay there."

"I understand." He gestured toward the map. "Come over here, and I'll show you how the fire has been contained so far."

On the map, Callie could see the fire road that wound up into the mountains, and then a smaller line that indicated the private road that led to the sanctuary. Several red and yellow flag pins marched alongside the road.

"What do these pins mean?" she asked.

"The red is where the fire is still active, and the yellow pins represent where we've suppressed the fire, but there still exists the potential for flames to ignite again." He indicated her father's property, which contained several yellow pins. "Because there's so much forest surrounding the sanctuary, we have a layer of needles, leaves, and dry vegetation on the ground.

"We call this material *duff*, which can smolder for days after a fire. Moreover, because it's burning in steep and rocky terrain, this fire is completely unpredictable. Until the crew has a chance to complete the mop-up operations, no one is going up there."

"What if some of your crew went with me?" Callie persisted, unwilling to give up so easily. "They can do their mop-up thing, while I get the wolves rounded up and into the kennel truck. Would that work?"

The Captain shook his head. "No, I'm sorry. We're anticipating gusty, west winds and dry conditions, which will likely push the fire to the north and east. This thing has scorched more than four thousand acres, and has transitioned to a Type 1 incident management team—the highest level of fire response. Types 1s are only called in for the most extreme situations, if that tells you anything. We have more than three hundred firefighting personnel working this fire, and it still has the potential to double in size every day that it burns." He was immovable. "So am I going to let you head into that? No way."

Callie thought of the wolves still at the sanctuary. They had come through the wildfire, but they still needed human intervention in order to survive. "Is there any possibility that your men could at least check on the animals, and ensure they have enough food and water?"

"I'll see what I can do," the captain finally said. "I have crews working on line construction south of your property. I'll have them check fire spread around the sanctuary. Is there any food on the premises for the wolves?"

"There's a concrete outbuilding that Tyler said is still intact, and there's food inside, but I'm not sure if it's still good."

Captain Gaskill was quiet for a moment, considering. "Bring a cooler of food by in the morning," he finally said, "and I'll make sure it gets to the wolves. If we can get ahead of the fire, you might be able to return to the sanctuary tomorrow, or the day after."

Callie nodded, and some of the tightness that had settled between her shoulder blades eased. She wouldn't relax until the wolves were safely removed from the sanctuary, but if the firefighters could bring them food and ensure they were okay, she could wait one or two more days to get back in and bring them out.

"Thanks," she said. "And please tell Tyler I said thank you, too."

Captain Gaskill gave her a speculative look, and one corner of his mouth turned up, as if amused. "Sure. See you tomorrow."

Callie walked back toward her truck, feeling his eyes on her. She skirted a group of men coming out of the campground shower facilities, and weaved her way through the maze of trailers and tents. The tourists were almost entirely absent now, with only a small cluster of campers at the far end of the campground. Once the wildfire was contained and the Way to the Sun Road reopened, the summer hordes would return.

As a child, Callie always wondered why the sanctuary was so far from town, where her father might have capitalized on the tourists who frequented the area. They would have paid good money to visit the sanctuary and view the wolves. As she grew older, she came to understand that her father didn't want tourists coming to the sanctuary. He disliked strangers tramping around the pens and stressing the wolves, and believed visitors to the sanctuary were an insurance liability. Only after her mother left them, did he break down and hire several assistants to help with the care of the wolves. Even that had been done reluctantly.

After Callie had left Montana to pursue her veterinary degree in California, Frank had slowly started extending invitations to the local schools to bring their students to the sanctuary for a day of awareness and understanding. The school field trips brought in a little extra money, but the biggest benefit was that they also resulted in additional donations from the local communities. Callie knew the residents of St. Mary and Browning viewed Frank as something of an eccentric, but they had always been good to him, checking on him during the extreme winter months, and helping him care for the wolves.

Now, with everything gone, he'd have no choice but to

return with her to California. She wouldn't give him a choice. As soon as he was strong enough to travel, they'd leave Montana for good.

TYLER WAS UP and dressed the following morning before the nurses made their first rounds. He felt pretty much back to normal, except for a residual wheezing when he drew in a deep breath. It was no big deal, and would clear up soon enough. He was anxious to get back to work. Twenty-four hours in a hospital had not been part of his plan, and he wasn't staying a second longer than he needed to.

Ace was waiting for him by the nurse's station as he came out of his room. He straightened as he saw Tyler. "Hey, bro." Ace greeted him. "You done being a skater? Ready to get back to work?"

A skater was a derogatory term for a lazy firefighter, so Tyler ignored the comment and continued walking past the nursing station. "I signed the discharge papers, but I have one thing I need to do before I leave. You can stay here, Romeo, or go pull a truck around and meet me out front."

Without waiting for Ace's response, he followed the signs to the cardiac unit, and located Frank McLain's room. He was no longer in the ICU, but in a shared room. Tyler stood in the doorway and looked at the man who lay sleeping in the nearest bed. The rhythmic beeping of the heart monitor and the soft whoosh of the oxygen machine were the only sounds. Frank's jaw was slack, and IV tubes protruded from his arm. He looked elderly and frail, and Tyler had a tough time picturing him fully recovered, never mind returning to the sanctuary to continue caring for the wolves. He bore no resemblance to the man who had grimly clung to the wire fencing of the enclosure, refusing to leave his property even in the face of a deadly wildfire.

As he turned away and made his way to where Ace waited for him, Tyler admitted he'd hoped to see Callie again before he left. She hadn't come by his room a second time yesterday, and he acknowledged some disappointment.

Ace was waiting for him in one of the Glacier Creek base pickup trucks, and Tyler climbed into the front seat.

"Where we headed?"

"Over to the incident command center," Ace replied. "We've got a couple of tents set up. I figure there are about a hundred or more response crews, but they have showers and grub."

"Are we jumping today?"

Ace shrugged. "I don't know. I haven't seen the list yet." He looked over at Tyler. "Sure you're ready?"

"I was born ready." Tyler quipped and then grew serious. "I feel good. I just pushed myself too hard, but I'm back."

He didn't want anyone thinking he couldn't do his job, or that he wasn't fully recovered. Smoke inhalation and heat exhaustion were job hazards. Most of the crew had suffered from one or the other during their firefighting career, but the experience had been a first for Tyler, and one he wasn't anxious to repeat.

"Some of the crew was trucked up into the mountains this morning." Ace offered.

Tyler's attention sharpened on the other man. "Oh yeah? So the access roads are open?"

"Seems so." Ace glanced over at him. "What are you thinking?"

"I'm not sure yet. Do you happen to know where Callie McLain is staying?"

This time, Ace grinned. "About a hundred yards from our command tent, dude. They gave her one of the cabins on the campground so she can be close to where they're bringing in the rescued animals. Did you know she's a vet?"

"A *veterinary physician*." He corrected. "Yeah, she mentioned that."

The knowledge that Callie might be at the incident command center caused a rush of anticipation. But if the access roads were open again, that meant the ground crews could handle the wildfire, and there might not even be a need for any more jumpers. If that was the case, they could be returning to Glacier Creek soon, and he might not even have the chance to see pretty Callie McLain again. He found the thought depressing.

CHAPTER EIGHT

C ALLIE SPENT THE day at the animal rescue tent, glad for the activity that kept her mind off the wolves…and Tyler Dodson. Was he recovering? Had they released him from the hospital? Would he come to the campground first, or head directly back into the teeth of the wildfire?

She crouched beside the dog that had been brought in two days earlier with burns and an infected bite wound. As she spoke gently to him, he lifted his head and licked her hand. They had named him Napi, which meant Old Man in the native Blackfeet language. So far, nobody had come forward to claim him. He was quickly becoming a favorite among the volunteers, with his gentle nature and happy spirit.

"C'mon, old man," she said, as he licked her hand. "Let's get you up onto the table and check your wound."

He pushed himself to his feet, and obediently followed her out of the wire pen and over to where the examination tables had been set up. Napi was still heavily bandaged, and still favored his injured leg. Callie might have been able to lift him herself, but didn't want to put any pressure on his injuries.

"Can I have a hand here, please?" she called out.

"Sure."

Callie snapped around at the sound of the deep voice, and found herself looking directly into Tyler's blue-green eyes, as he bent and easily lifted the dog onto the table. Her pulse quickened and gladness surged through her. She hadn't thought she would see him again, and certainly not so soon. The knowledge he'd sought her out made her want to dance.

"Hey." She greeted him, hoping her voice didn't betray her pleasure. "Should you be out of the hospital so soon?"

He kept one hand firmly on the dog's ruff to prevent him from jumping down and grinned at her. "I'm good. How're you doing?"

His eyes swept over her, missing nothing, and Callie was aware of how she must look. Wearing jeans and an old jersey, with her hair scraped back into a ponytail, Callie was pretty sure she couldn't look any less attractive.

"I'm okay." She grimaced. "Not looking too glam, but that comes with the territory, I guess."

Keeping one hand on the dog, Tyler spread his other arm and looked down at himself in cheerful deprecation. "Trust me, I get it. This is about as glam as I get, even on a good day."

Instead of putting her at ease, all he did was draw her attention to his amazing physique. His tee shirt was faded and worn, and sported a couple of frayed holes across his rugged shoulders, and his arms bulged with muscles. Beneath the soft fabric, she could see a hint of washboard abs. The rugged nylon belt, threaded through the loopholes on his cargo pants, only drew her attention to his trim waist and lean hips.

"Yeah," she said sarcastically, "you look really terrible."

"So what's going on with this guy?" he asked, turning his attention to the dog on the table, and gently ruffling his fur.

Callie dragged her own attention away from Tyler and bent over the dog. "This is Napi. He was brought in a couple of days ago with burns, and what looked like a bite wound on his leg." She stroked the dog's neck. "But he's a fighter, and he'll be fine in a couple of weeks." She rubbed behind his ears. "Won't you, my handsome boy?"

"Anything I can help you with?" Tyler asked.

"Sure. If you don't mind holding him while I check his bandages, that would be great."

Callie was acutely aware of Tyler's big hands holding the dog, while she carefully unwound the gauze and checked Napi's injuries. As she applied more ointment, he stroked the dog and spoke gently to it, soothing it.

"You're a natural at this." She smiled, reapplying fresh bandages. "Maybe you missed your calling."

Tyler helped lift the dog from the table, and watched as she walked Napi back to his enclosure. "Animals like me," he said when she returned. "And I tend to like them. Most of them anyway."

She gave him an inquiring look as she peeled off her exam gloves, and put away her supplies. "What does that mean?"

"I came across a grizzly bear once, while I was hiking through the park. Thankfully, it was October, and this guy was getting ready to hibernate, so he wasn't hungry and he wasn't too interested in me."

"You're lucky," she said. "I met a man once, when I was a kid, who'd survived a grizzly attack." She gave a shiver of recollection. "It wasn't pretty."

"It never is."

She leaned back against the table and looked at him. In her medical opinion, he still looked tired, and she thought he might have benefitted from another day of rest but, overall, he looked a lot better than he had the last two times she'd seen him. His eyes were clear, and now that he was no longer covered in soot and dirt, she could see how handsome he really was. She'd thought his face was hard, but when he looked at her like he was doing now, all she felt was awareness. Of him.

Of herself.

"So, I went over and talked to your captain this morning," she said in a rush. "He thought there might be a chance I could return to the sanctuary in the next day or so."

"That's actually why I'm here," he said. "The access road has been reopened, and we need to bring some supplies up to the guys who are working the construction line." He folded his arms across his chest, which only made his shoulders and arms seem even bigger. "I thought we could bring your truck, and try to get the wolves out of there."

"Are you serious? Oh, Tyler, thank you!"

Before she could think twice, she pushed herself away from the table and gave him a swift hug. His arms came around her, and she found herself pressed up against all that solid warmth, with his surprised laughter huffing into her hair. He smelled good, like clean male, and his arms felt wonderful around her.

"Wow," he said, his voice a rough rasp against her ear. "You're welcome."

Stepping back, Callie self-consciously tucked a loose strand of hair behind her ear. "Thank you. It's just that I've been so worried, and it didn't seem like I was going to be able to get back there anytime soon, and the fact that you're willing to go with me—" She broke off, aware she was babbling. "Thank you."

He inclined his head. "You're very welcome." He glanced at his watch, a rugged sports model with a durable nylon strap. "I have some stuff I need to go over with the boss, so why don't I meet you back here in an hour? Does that give you enough time to get whatever it is you need?"

Callie nodded, smiling. "Yes. Absolutely. I'll see you in an hour."

She watched as he walked away, admiring his easy, loose-limbed stride. He seemed to know most of the other rescue personnel at the campground, and stopped frequently to exchange a greeting or a handshake. Callie gave herself a mental kick and turned away, determined not to stare after him until he was gone. He was way too sexy for her peace of mind. She shouldn't even be interested in him, because what was the point? Once the wildfire was under control he'd return to Glacier Creek, which was easily a three hour drive from St. Mary, provided the park road was open, and she didn't have to take the longer route around the perimeter. Not that she intended to stick around.

She'd stay just long enough to get her father back on his feet, and then she'd bring him with her to California. She had no intention of staying in Montana. As far as she was concerned, there was nothing here for her, at least not long-term, and she was pretty sure guys like Tyler Dodson didn't do long-term, anyway. Or long distance.

Nope, like the wildfires he fought, it was best to keep a safe distance, or she might find herself badly burned.

TYLER SAT IN the cab of the kennel truck with Callie as they followed the supply convoy up the access road toward the sanctuary. She'd loaded some emergency medical supplies into the truck, along with a five-gallon pail of raw meat and three catchpoles.

Tyler was accustomed to seeing the ravages of wildfire, but he could see how much Callie was affected by the sight of the charred, blackened trees that lined either side of the road, for as far as they could see. Every so often, plumes of smoke spiraled upward out of the ground, evidence of smoldering duff. When that happened, the convoy stopped and a couple of guys jumped out to dig up the area, kicking it over with enough dirt to ensure any live coals were smothered.

When they reached the intersection where the private road leading to the sanctuary branched off to the right, one truck continued straight, and the second truck turned toward her father's property.

"We thought it best to bring a truck with us," Tyler explained. "That way, if there are any spot fires still burning, we can take care of those while you round up the animals."

Tyler could have handled it on his own, but Sam had been adamant that two others go with them to the sanctuary. Ace and Vin had volunteered, and now Callie followed their vehicle up the winding road.

"My God," she breathed, peering through the windshield. "There's nothing left."

The road opened into a clearing that had once been the sanctuary. Where the house had once stood, there was now only the freestanding, stone fireplace, surrounded by a pile of blackened rubble. The forest behind the house looked skeletal, and the dense underbrush that had surrounded the property was gone. Only the concrete outbuilding remained, with its twisted, metal roof.

"The pens are intact," Tyler reminded her. "Your father

was smart to build everything out of metal, including the posts."

"That was Randy's idea," she murmured, still staring in horror at the devastation. "I just can't believe everything is gone. I mean, I knew it was gone, but it's not the same as *seeing* it gone."

Her hands gripped the steering wheel so tightly that her knuckles had turned white. Reaching over, Tyler covered one of her hands with his own. "C'mon," he urged quietly. "Let's get the wolves and get the hell out of here. There's nothing left here for you, or your dad."

She turned to him, her face reflecting her loss. "You're right. There's nothing left."

Pulling her hand free, she climbed out of the truck and went around to the back to retrieve the supplies she had brought. Tyler got out and went to join Ace and Vin, who were surveying the damage and kicking at ground with their boots.

"Looks okay up here," Vin commented. "I don't see any visible hot spots, but we'll take a walk around just to be sure. You two okay?" He glanced over at Callie as she stalked toward the enclosures, the bucket of raw meat in one hand and a catchpole in the other.

"Fine," she said.

Tyler watched her, so determined to be strong, and felt a grudging respect for her. It couldn't be easy to see the house and property completely destroyed. Even if she could rebuild, it would take years for the landscape to recover.

As she made her way toward the back of the first pen, Tyler climbed into the truck and backed it up so it was as close to the enclosure as possible. Without the underbrush and dense forest to conceal them, he could see the bunkers in each pen, barely visible above the blackened earth. He climbed out of the truck and stood with Vin and Ace, watching as Callie approached the first bunker, talking in a low, soothing voice. She pulled a hunk of raw meat out of the bucket and tossed it onto the scorched ground, and then waited.

As they watched, an animal crept out of the bunker, slinking low, with its belly close to the ground. The wolf cautiously sniffed the meat, and then made a movement as if it would snatch the food and drag it back into the safety of the bunker. But before that could happen, Callie slipped the catchpole neatly over the animal's head. The wolf startled and tried to jerk back, and for a moment Tyler thought Callie would be pulled off her feet. But she dug in her heels and held on, and slowly walked the resistant wolf across the enclosure, until they reached the kennel truck. With surprising deftness, she put the frightened animal into one of the cages, and threw a hunk of meat in with him.

"I'm impressed," Ace said. "Wolf-girl really knows what she's doing."

Vin chuckled and clapped the younger man on the shoulder. "Okay, show's over. C'mon, tenderfoot, let me show you how to do mop-up."

"Hey, in case you missed the memo, I don't think I qualify as a rookie anymore," Ace protested, as he followed Vin. "I've got almost two dozen jumps under my belt now."

Tyler shifted his attention back to Callie and watched as she patiently coaxed the remaining wolves out of their dens. The lure of fresh meat and water was pretty good incentive for them to come out, but Tyler suspected she had something to do with it, too. The wolves knew her scent; they trusted her. Except for the first wolf, none of the animals resisted when she led them to the kennel truck.

Tyler scrubbed a hand over the back of his head as he watched her work. He had hung back to keep an eye on her in case any of the wolves gave her trouble. But there was another reason he remained near; he wanted to watch her because she was beautiful, and smart, and there was a quality about her that he found very appealing.

She had transferred five wolves to the kennel truck and had returned for the sixth, when he suddenly heard her cry out, and he realized he could no longer see her inside the enclosure.

"Callie?" He strode along the perimeter of the pen, trying to locate her. "Callie, answer me! Where are you?"

As he peered through the wire fencing, he finally saw her crawling on her hands and knees out of the concrete bunker. Without hesitation, he sprinted back to the gate and slipped inside, running over to where she sat, desolate, on the blackened ground.

He crouched beside her, trying to see her face. "What is it? Are you bitten? Are you hurt?"

She shook her head. "No."

Tyler looked from her, to the entrance of the bunker, and started to climb inside.

"No!" Callie grabbed his arm and pulled him back. "Don't go in there, at least not until I bring Kobo out."

Tyler stared at the entrance. From deep inside the bunker, he heard a low, mournful keening. He frowned and looked back at Callie. "Is there an injured wolf in there?"

She shook her head, but when she raised her face to his, he could see tears had created pale streaks through the soot on her cheeks.

"Sorry." She managed and dragged her sleeve across her eyes. "You'd think after all these years, I'd get used to animals reaching the end of their lives, but this one—" She made a choking sound. "This one just got to me."

"Hey, no, don't apologize," Tyler said, still trying to figure out what was going on. He listened to the low wail. "Is that a wolf dying? Because I'll help you bring it out; we can get it back to St. Mary. Maybe it's not too late."

"No, it's definitely too late," Callie confirmed. "Nina, our oldest wolf, didn't survive. Her body is in there, and that's her mate, Kobo, mourning her."

Tyler rocked back on his heels as he digested this. "Okay. So we need to bring them both out."

Her expression registered her surprise. "Yes."

"So which would be easier? To bring Nina out first, or Kobo?"

Callie pushed herself to her feet, and Tyler rose to stand beside her. "I don't think Kobo will let me touch her," she said. "We'll have to entice him out first."

"Tell me what to do."

"He's hungry. I think he'll come out if I offer him some food. Once I catch him up, could you go in and bring Nina out? I don't think I can do it."

"Sure." The sadness of her expression as she talked about the wolf was almost more than he could stand. "Hey, come here."

Before she could protest, he pulled her into his arms. For just an instant she stood stiff and awkward in his embrace, and then she relaxed against him, as if all the strength had suddenly been drained out of her. Tyler's arms tightened reflexively, and a surge of protectiveness nearly swamped him. Her hair was silky against his chin, and he breathed in her clean fragrance.

"I'm sorry." She repeated, her voice muffled against his shirt. "I'm not usually this emotional, but it's been a rough week."

"Shh, I'm here for you," he found himself saying. "It'll be okay."

She nodded, and after a moment, slowly pulled away from his embrace. She didn't meet his eyes, but he didn't miss her heightened color.

"I'll bring Kobo out," she said, and turned away to retrieve the bucket of meat, and the catchpole.

As she gently enticed Kobo from the bunker, and expertly moved him to the kennel truck, Tyler couldn't help but admire how the animals responded to her. As wild and untamed as they were, they trusted her. He felt an affinity with the wolves, recognizing that there was something special about Callie. For just a moment, he wondered if she might not be capable of domesticating him, too.

CHAPTER NINE

"Y OU DID A good job back there," Tyler said, as she drove the kennel truck through the pass and back toward St. Mary. "I'm sorry about Nina."

Callie nodded and her hands tightened on the steering wheel. "Thank you. She was very old, and the wildfire was just too much for her." She glanced at him. "Most people think wolves are tough, but they can actually become stressed very easily."

"Will Kobo be okay?"

Callie thought of the mournful sounds the wolf had made while watching over Nina's body. Few people understood the strong bonds that wolves developed, or how they mourned the passing of a pack member.

"I hope so. We found a wolf sanctuary in Wyoming, willing to take the wolves in. So once he settles in and gets evaluated, he has a good chance of being placed with another female."

Callie had called Randy as soon as she'd loaded the six wolves into the kennel truck, and he'd volunteered to make the long, eight hundred-mile drive to Cheyenne. He would leave as soon they arrived in St. Mary, in order to reduce the time the wolves would have to spend in the truck. Once they reached Cheyenne, the animals would receive a complete checkup, and be placed with their pack mates in new enclosures. Their new home would be permanent; they wouldn't return to Montana.

Callie hadn't been kidding when she'd told Tyler it had been a rough week. Between her father's health, losing the ranch, and trying to find new homes for the wolves, she felt more stressed than she could ever recall. She still hadn't told her father that all of the wolves had been placed in new homes, or that there was no chance he could reopen the sanctuary. She wasn't sure he would forgive her.

She thought again of the spontaneous hug Tyler had given her. The gesture had been so unexpected that for a moment, she'd been too shocked to react. Then she'd become acutely conscious of how good his arms felt around her, of his scent, and his strength. Part of her wanted to press closer to him, and never leave. She wanted to lean on him; let him take care of her. Of everything.

What had he said?

I'm here for you.

Realistically, she knew that wasn't true, since he'd likely return to Glacier Creek within the next day or so, and she wouldn't be here for any longer than absolutely necessary. But she appreciated his kindness, and told herself it was perfectly normal for her to be attracted to him—he was a rugged, good-looking man, capable of kind acts. In fact, he was pretty perfect. She'd tried to find some fault in him, but so far hadn't come up with anything. The fact he would be leaving St. Mary soon was probably a good thing, since she suspected he was the kind of guy a girl could easily fall for.

For all she knew, he was already taken—it seemed as if all the good guys were. Callie found the thought depressing, and cast a furtive glance at his hands. He was checking his cell phone for messages, and she couldn't help but notice how strong and capable his hands looked. He wore no rings, and she couldn't see any telltale indent on his ring finger.

"So, you must be pretty anxious to get back to Glacier Creek," she commented, striving for a casual tone. "I'm sure your wife worries about you when you're gone."

He slanted her an amused look, as if he saw through her transparent attempt for information. "No wife, no fiancée, no girlfriend," he replied, before returning his attention to his messages. "Not yet."

Was it her imagination, or was there an implied promise in his words? Something fluttered in Callie's stomach. What would it be like to be Tyler Dodson's girlfriend?

Amazing.

Overwhelming.

He was an extremely physical man, and she imagined that would extend to his intimate relationships, as well. And suddenly, she could picture it so clearly that treacherous heat unfurled low in her abdomen, rushing to her sex so she had to resist the urge to squirm in her seat. Desperate to think about something other than Tyler, naked and covering her, she grasped at the first topic that sprang to mind.

"How much of the wildfire has been contained, so far?"

"There's going to be a public meeting tonight at the incident command center," he replied. "But the fire is about sixty-five percent contained. I've been doing this for a long time, and I've never seen a wildfire as crazy and unpredictable as this one, but I think it's safe to say we'll wrap up in a day or so."

"So soon?" She blurted the words without thinking, even though she'd told herself to expect this.

He shifted his attention from the road to her, and Callie felt warm color sweep into her face. Nothing like being obvious.

"You know I can't stay," he said quietly.

And there it was again, the intense awareness that made her skin tingle and her stomach tighten into knots.

"I know," she said, nodding, and dragged her attention back to the road. "It's just that you've been so great, helping me with the wolves, and I feel partly responsible for you ending up in the hospital."

Liar.

It's just that I want you.

"Don't. It's a job hazard, and it won't be the last time I overdo it during a deployment. As for the wolves, you know I'm happy to help you."

"Still, I'd like to do something to repay you," she insisted. "Maybe dinner at the Black Bear Grill?"

Tyler laughed. "Thanks, but I'm not exactly equipped to go anywhere civilized, especially not a restaurant." He was quiet for a moment. "How about you come over to our base camp tonight, and I'll grill you a couple of hotdogs? It won't be fancy, but it's probably better than anything the hospital cafeteria could offer. Trust me—I know."

How did he know she'd been eating her meals at the hospital, in between visits with her father? The thought of sitting with all those smokejumpers made her nervous, but the lure of spending a little more time with Tyler was too irresistible to turn down.

"Alright," she conceded. "I need to check on my dad, first. Are you sure I won't be intruding?"

"Trust me," he said drily, "you won't be intruding. Tonight's our only night away from the front line of the fire, to give us a chance to catch some sleep and maybe a shower. Your being there will be a welcome change from sitting around, staring at each other."

Callie drew in a breath. "Okay, then. It's a date."

She instantly regretted her choice of words when Tyler's expression remained impassive. Biting her lip, she focused on her driving, grateful when they reached the turnoff to St. Mary. She had agreed to meet Randy at the campground, and as they pulled into the field, she spotted his pickup truck.

They climbed out of the truck, and Callie saw that Randy had Sara, her father's second assistant, with him. They had been leaning against the hood of the truck when they pulled up. They straightened and stepped away as Callie approached, but not before she saw them holding hands. She'd no idea the two were romantically involved, although it made sense. They spent a lot of time working together with the wolves. They were both in their early thirties, and while Randy looked like a lumberjack with his dark beard and powerful shoulders, Sara was his complete opposite in every way. Petite and blonde, with skintight jeans and western boots, she looked as if she would be more comfortable on the dance floor of a country-western bar. But Callie had seen her working at the sanctuary. Not only was she patient and caring with the wolves, but she had a lighthearted nature and enjoyed nothing more than teasing Randy. Now Callie introduced Tyler to them, seeing the lively interest in Sara's eyes.

"So you're the firefighter who helped Callie save the wolves, huh?" she asked, running her gaze over him in blatant appreciation. "Makes me wish I'd stuck around that morning."

"I'm right here," Randy reminded her, his tone dry.

"Yes, but this guy specializes in putting out fires," she quipped. "You know, find 'em hot and leave 'em wet? Can you say the same?"

Callie barely contained her shocked laugh. Randy glowered at Sara, and stomped around to the driver's side of the kennel truck. "It's a long drive to Cheyenne; I should get going."

Sara grinned, and reaching into the bed of Randy's truck, withdrew a large cooler, and several jugs of water. "I'll just grab these," she said brightly.

Before she could muscle the cooler out of the bed, Randy was right there, taking it from her. "I've got it," he said gruffly. "Are you coming with me, or would you rather stay here with the fire extinguisher?"

"Hmmm," she said, and let her gaze slide over Tyler again, as if seriously considering it.

Callie liked Sara, but felt herself going tense as she watched the other woman size Tyler up. For his part, Tyler merely smiled politely, and reached past her for the jugs of water, lifting three in each hand as if they weighed nothing.

"Get in the truck," Randy said to Sara, tossing the cooler and the jugs of water into the seat behind the cab.

"Randy, before you leave, can you do me a favor?" Callie asked.

"Sure, what's up?"

Callie explained about Nina, and how they had placed her body into one of the crates. "Could you bring her over to Shayla? She'll take care of her."

Once the arrangements for Nina had been made, Randy and Sara left, promising to contact them once they reached Wyoming.

"Sorry about that," Callie said. "Sara can be a little outspoken, and she likes to get Randy going, even at the expense of other people."

"No problem," Tyler replied, his mouth curving. "I've heard it all before. Where are you staying?"

Callie indicated the row of small, rustic cabins near the lake. "I'm staying there for now."

Tyler nodded. "Do you have everything you need?"

"I didn't bring much with me from California. Just a suitcase, and I was able to throw that into the truck before we left the sanctuary, along with some of my dad's things."

Beside her, Tyler stilled.

"I thought you were from St. Mary." His voice was cautious.

"Originally, yes. But I went to veterinary school in California, and I've lived in Monterey for the past eight years." She looked at him, wondering why his expression had suddenly gone tight. "Why?"

He shrugged. "Nothing."

But Callie had the distinct sense he'd suddenly withdrawn from her. Was it because she was from California? Had he believed that she lived in Montana? Had he hoped they might see each other after he returned to Glacier Creek? Even if she lived in St. Mary, it was easily a two-hour drive to Glacier Creek, through Glacier National Park. In the winter, when the mountain passes were closed, that drive became five hours to circle around the park, using the interstate.

"Okay." She pushed her hands into the pockets of her jeans. "So, I guess I'll go grab a shower, stop by the hospital, and then go over to the rescue area and check on my four-legged patients." She hesitated. "Thanks again for all your help today, Ty. With everything. I sort of lost it a little bit, and you were really nice about it, so thank you. A lot of guys would have run in the other direction."

"Yeah, well, those guys would be idiots. I don't scare easily." His manner was still remote, and his expression had lost the warmth it usually held when he looked at her. "So, I'll see you around six? Which cabin are you in? I'll come over and get you."

Callie didn't know if he really wanted to see her that night, or if he was just being polite. His whole posture had become a little bit aloof, which made her uncertain.

"You know," she began cautiously, "if you've changed your mind, it's fine. Please don't feel as if you need to take care of me. I can grab something to eat at the hospital. Really."

To her surprise, he stepped close to her, until she felt overwhelmed by his sheer physicality.

"Is that what you think?" he asked, his voice low and gruff. "That I've changed my mind?"

"Well, have you?" Callie refused to be intimidated by his closeness, and tipped her head back to look directly into his eyes, which was a huge mistake. The expression in those blue-green depths was enough to make her breath hitch, and her toes curl inside her boots.

"I have not," he said firmly. "I'll come by at six to get you."

"Okay." Was that her voice that sounded so breathy? "See you then."

She walked away, in the direction of the cabins, conscious that he might be watching her. She had to resist the urge to glance back over her shoulder, but couldn't prevent a wide smile at the knowledge he wanted to see her again. So maybe they couldn't pursue anything serious, given how far apart they lived, but for now at least, she intended to enjoy whatever time they might have.

CHAPTER TEN

"WHAT'S GOING ON?" Vin asked, as Tyler joined him and the rest of the crew at the smokejumper tent later that afternoon. "Feeling better after your siesta at the hospital? Or is that just how you're meeting chicks these days?"

"I'm good," Tyler said, ignoring the jibe. "What's the latest?"

"We won't be jumping this fire again," Vin said, sounding disappointed. "We contained it above the access roads, and the ground crews said they'll have it completely suppressed within the next forty-eight hours."

"So when are we headed back?"

"Tomorrow. You sure you're okay? You don't look it."

Tyler shrugged, and helped himself to a bottle of water from one of the coolers that lined the perimeter of the tent. "I was hoping to spend some more time here, that's all."

Ace lifted his head from where he and Liam had been studying a fire map. "What's this? Tough guy has a thing for wolf-girl? And here I thought you were a confirmed bachelor. You're all about the job and shit, as least that's what you've always said." He dropped his head into his hands in exaggerated dismay. "Man, am I disappointed."

"I get it," Vin said, ignoring Ace. "She's pretty, she's got a great bod, and she seems nice."

"She is," Tyler replied. "But it's a bad idea, and I should just keep the hell away."

But he sounded unconvinced, even to his own ears.

"What, is she married?"

"No, worse." Tyler grimaced. "She lives in California."

"Ah." Vin was silent for a moment. "That's definitely a game changer. Could even be a deal breaker, if she's got her heart set on staying there."

Ace leaned forward. "Wait, are you serious? You like her that much? You don't even know her."

And that was the problem.

Tyler hadn't known Alicia very well, either, when he'd asked her to marry him. If he had, he would have realized she wasn't cut out for life in Montana. Not that he was even close to considering marriage again. But it would be almost impossible to get to know Callie if she was living out on the west coast, and he was in Montana. And he knew enough about himself to know that he could never be happy anywhere else. He thought about the acreage he'd purchased on the north ridge, with views of Flathead Lake and Swan Peak. He'd had plans drawn up for a sprawling timber frame house, and he couldn't wait to break ground on the project.

"We'll see what happens," he said, noncommittal. "I invited her to eat with us tonight."

This was met with hoots and some ribald comments. As one of the oldest members of the smokejumping crew, Tyler had been a bachelor for longer than some of the guys had been at the base. Moreover, he almost never brought women home with him. He liked spending time at The Drop Zone pub, but it was more for the company of his smokejumping pals. He'd had plenty of invitations from the women who frequented the bar, but it had been a long time since he'd accepted one.

Callie didn't strike him as the kind of woman who did casual hookups, and there was a part of him that was glad about that. The likelihood he would end up hurting her was greater if they slept together. She was right about one thing—he regretted inviting her to the camp. He told himself he only needed to get through tonight, and then he would stay away from her. With everything she had going on in her life, she probably wouldn't even notice when he made a quiet exit.

"Well, your mother is going to be real happy if this thing works out," Vin said cheerfully. "She's been dropping hints about grandchildren for years."

"I'll be sorry to disappoint her," Tyler said smoothly. "Look, I only asked Callie to come grab a bite with us, so she wouldn't have to spend another evening by herself. She's been through a lot, her father is in the hospital, and I don't think she has too many friends here in St. Mary." He shrugged. "It's not a big deal."

Vin gave him a knowing look. "Sure," he agreed, but he didn't sound convinced.

TYLER KNOCKED ON the door of Callie's cabin at six o'clock, and she opened it almost immediately. She wore a sleeveless cotton dress in a floral fabric, paired with cowboy boots that showed off her slender legs. Her hair was loose around her face, and tiny, silver disks winked on each earlobe. For a moment, Tyler couldn't stop himself from staring. He'd known she was pretty, but tonight she looked sweet and soft, and utterly feminine.

"Hi." She greeted him. She held a light sweater in her hands, and now she clutched it against her chest. "Are you sure about this?"

"Absolutely."

He waited while she closed the door, and then fell into step beside him as they made their way across the field to where the smokejumper base camp was located.

"Are you doing okay?" he asked. "Your dad is still recovering?"

She nodded and tucked a strand of dark hair behind one ear. "Yes, he's as well as can be expected. The doctors said they'll keep him for another week, and then he should be well enough to move to a rehab center."

"That's good news."

She gave a small sigh. "You're right. It is good news, and

I'm so glad he's on the mend, but I just don't know if I can stick around for another two to three weeks. I've already been gone longer than I'd planned."

"There's nobody else who can come and look after him until he's released?"

"No. He and my mom divorced when I was thirteen. She lives in California, too, and they don't really get along."

Tyler sensed that was a huge understatement, but it made sense why she had settled on the west coast.

"What does your mother do?"

"She teaches middle school math and science."

"That's impressive. I thought you needed a black belt in karate to handle middle-schoolers."

Callie laughed. "Well, she doesn't have a black belt, but I think she holds her own. She loves what she does. She used to teach at the elementary school in Browning, before her and my dad split up."

"Really? Did you ever have her for a teacher?"

"No, and I'm not sure I would have wanted to be in her class. I think she would have been tougher on me than the rest of the kids, just to prove she wasn't giving me any preferential treatment."

Tyler thought of all the firefighting qualification courses he'd taken, where his stepfather had been the instructor. He certainly couldn't accuse Mike Eldridge of giving him special treatment. Even when Tyler had aced every exam, and passed every physical requirement with flying colors, all he'd received was a grunt of acknowledgment. At the time, it had really bothered him. As he grew older, he told himself it didn't matter if he had Mike's approval. He had a good life. Had he made his share of mistakes? Hell, yeah, but he'd also learned from them. Which was why he didn't plan on getting married again.

But that didn't mean he couldn't enjoy spending time with Callie while he was in St. Mary. Watching her talk, he wondered what it would be like to really kiss her, to feel those soft lips beneath his own. Her arms were slim and toned, and she had a habit of tucking her hair behind her ear, even when there weren't any loose strands. Tyler found the gesture both endearing and sexy.

They had reached the tent where most of the smoke-jumper crew was sitting around a fire pit. A propane grill had been set up nearby, and Garrett Broxson was flipping burgers, hotdogs, and brats. Someone had dragged a folding table out of the tent, and Greg Winters was prepping rolls and condiments. Vin and Ace rose to their feet to greet Callie, and Tyler quickly made the introductions to the crew.

"Sit here," Ace said, indicating the camp chair he had just vacated. "I promised Garrett I'd give him a hand with the grill."

Greg handed her a cold bottle of water, and Tyler made himself comfortable on a rustic log bench that sat near the fire pit. He watched as Callie talked with the guys, laughing at their stories and their jokes, and sharing some of her own, mostly to do with the wolves, or some of the funnier things she'd seen while working as a vet.

After they'd eaten, and the sun had dropped below the mountains behind them, some of the married crew said good-night, and left to bunk down in the nearby tents. The remaining guys talked quietly together, or checked their cell phones for messages.

"Can I help clean up?" Callie asked.

"Absolutely not," Vin said. "You're a guest tonight."

"There's no need," Tyler assured her. "We've done this so many times that we have it down to a science." He stood up, and took her hand, pulling her to her feet. "Besides, there's nothing left to clean up. Everything is disposable. Why don't we walk down to the water?"

"Okay." She glanced at the men who still sat talking by the fire. "Are you sure we're not being rude?"

Tyler drew her away from the group and leaned down to speak into her ear. "If we don't leave now, I can't guarantee that *they* won't become rude, or at least do their best to embarrass us."

Callie smiled, and Tyler kept her hand in his as he led her away from the incident command post and toward the lake, where the shadows were deeper.

"So this is it," she said, when they reached the edge of the lake. "Your last night in St. Mary."

"Yes. We'll head back to Glacier Creek before noon tomorrow."

"Seems so strange," she mused. "I didn't think I'd get used to the sound of the helicopters scooping water out of the lake, but it's so quiet now that I almost miss the noise."

"The meteorologists are calling for rain over the next couple of days, which will help suppress what's left of the fire," he said. "The ground crews here can manage any remaining spot fires that crop up, so there's no sense in us staying."

"Everyone is talking about what a crazy fire season this has been, so I'm sure you'll be heading out to fight another fire before too long."

"I'm counting on it," he said. "Both California and Alaska are having record wildfire seasons, and it's still early. If I had to guess, I'd say we won't be spending too much time in Glacier Creek this summer. We'll probably jump our next fire in the next day or two."

The water on the lake was calm, and Tyler could see the lights from the campground reflected on its surface. Overhead, the stars were just beginning to appear, and he noted with satisfaction there wasn't any smoke to diminish their brilliance. The temperatures had cooled a bit, and he could feel the increasing humidity in the air.

Spotting a large rock near the edge of the water, he sat down on it and pulled Callie down beside him. Water lapped at the base of the rock, and Tyler leaned down to unlace his boots and kick them off, before peeling his socks off and stuffing them inside the boots. He submerged his feet in the water, and let out a groan of delight.

Beside him, Callie giggled. "Feel good?"

"Oh, man, it feels so good." He rolled up the bottom of his cargo pants, and swished his feet back and forth. "C'mon, girl, kick off those boots and get your toes wet."

There wasn't a lot of room on the rock and when she bent forward to remove her boots, she almost lost her balance. She gave a small cry of alarm, and Tyler instinctively put his arm around her, steadying her.

"I've got you."

Laughing, she bent forward and pulled her boots off, and tossed them onto the grass behind them.

"Okay, here goes." She dipped her feet into the water, tentatively swirling them in small circles. "You're right, that does feel good."

Tyler had to agree—she felt nice, tucked against his side. Their feet slid against each other in the water and she relaxed fractionally, leaning into him. A light, floral fragrance clung to her hair, and Tyler had to resist the urge to bend his head and inhale her scent.

"So, what do you do in the winter, when there are no fires to fight?" she asked, tucking her chin into her shoulder as she looked at him. The movement put her mouth temptingly close to his, and he had to look away in order to focus on what she was saying, and not kiss her.

"I'm on call during the winter months, but I mostly work at Big Mountain."

"Oh! As what…a lift operator?"

Tyler felt a smile tug his mouth. "Uh, no. I'm national ski patrol. I monitor snow conditions, do mountain rescues, and generally keep the trails safe for the skiers, and when I'm not doing that, I'm a ski patrol instructor."

He could see she was impressed. "Wow. From one extreme to the other! Fire in the summer and ice in the winter."

"Yes, ma'am. I get to indulge two of my favorite activities—skydiving and skiing, *and* get paid for it. You can't ask for more than that. Do you ski?"

"Occasionally," she said. "I used to go when I was a kid. And I went out to Vail a couple of times last winter with a group of friends, but it's not something I do on a regular basis." She pulled a face. "We don't get much snow in Monterey."

"Well, you'll have to come out to Whitefish during the winter, and I'll take you up on the slopes. The view from the top is incredible. Skiing some of those trails is almost as exhilarating as jumping out of a plane," he said.

"Do you ever worry about the danger you face, when you jump into a wildfire?" Callie asked.

Tyler thought for a minute. "I'd be lying if I said I don't worry. But I worry more about the rest of the crew than I do about myself."

"Have you ever been hurt?"

"A couple of times, but nothing serious. I got hung up in

a tree once and busted my arm. Another time, when I was still a rookie, I landed badly and dislocated my shoulder."

She shivered, and Tyler reflexively tightened his arm around her. "I would worry so much if you were—"

She broke off abruptly, and Tyler wondered what she had been going to say. *If you were mine?*

"We take recertification courses all the time," he reassured her. "We practice, and we have safety protocols in place, and, most importantly, we look out for each other."

"But have you ever lost a crew member?"

Tyler thought of that awful day when Russ Edwards, their former captain, had crashed into a tree during a jump, and died. They'd lost more than a crew member that day. They'd lost both a friend and a mentor.

"Yes," he finally responded. "But we all know the risks, and we do everything we can to mitigate them. When accidents happen, we use them as a learning tool and try to prevent it happening again."

"How much longer do you think you'll do this?" She looked at him, her expression somber.

He blew out a hard breath, considering. "Well, I'm thirty-five. I've been fighting wildfires since before I graduated from high school. It's all I know. I hope to do it for at least another ten years."

"But isn't there an age limit, or something?"

Tyler gave a surprised laugh. "Are you saying I'm old?"

"No! Of course not." She sounded mortified. "Look at

you! You're thirty-five and you could probably run circles around guys who are half your age!"

"Thanks," he said drily. "We undergo periodic physical fitness and medical tests, and as long as we can pass those, we can jump."

He didn't add the physical fitness test was extremely arduous, and performed under rigorous conditions. He'd never had a problem exceeding the requirements, and even during the off-season, made sure he stayed in top shape. He knew guys, like his stepfather, who had jumped well into their forties.

"And you don't mind being gone so much?" she asked. "What does that kind of lifestyle do to personal relationships?"

"About what you'd expect," he said wryly. "Some of the guys are married, but a lot of us are divorced."

She looked sharply at him. "You're divorced?"

The night was growing dark, and he could no longer read her expression, but he heard the surprise in her voice.

"It was a long time ago," he said quietly. "We were both very young. It was a mistake. Thankfully, we didn't add to that mistake by having kids."

"I'm sorry."

"No, don't be." He didn't want to talk about himself, or his past relationships. "What about you? There's no animal doctor waiting for you back in California?"

Callie shook her head. "Nope, it's just me."

"What, are the men in California blind, or just stupid?"

Callie laughed. "I spend a lot of time at work, and I'm not really into the bar scene, so if I haven't met anyone I only have myself to blame."

"You like living in California?"

"It's okay." She tipped her face up to study the stars. "There was a time I couldn't wait to get out of Montana. I thought it was too cold, too isolated, too backwoods. I wanted sunshine and warmth, and a Starbucks within walking distance. But I've never seen stars like this in Monterey."

They were silent for several, long moments as they looked at the sky. Tyler could feel the rise and fall of each breath she took, the whisper of her hair against his cheek as a soft breeze stirred it. He suddenly wished he wasn't returning to Glacier Creek the next day. But he'd told the truth when he'd said they would likely deploy again within the next forty-eight hours. That was the nature of the job during the fire season.

"So I guess your job doesn't really allow for personal relationships, huh?" she asked.

Tyler knew she was hoping for some affirmation from him, but he couldn't make any promises, and he didn't want to mislead her.

"I'd say it's not exactly conducive to long-term commitments, but some of the guys on the crew have made it work." He paused. "But it's usually a little easier if both people live in the same state."

Callie drew in a deep breath, and gently pulled away

from him. She stood up, and walked a few steps away and stood looking out over the water, hugging her arms around her middle.

"This is crazy," he heard her say.

Rising to his feet, Tyler went and stood behind her. He put his hands on her shoulders and pulled her back against his chest, crossing his own arms over hers. Her head rested just beneath his chin, and he finally gave in to the urge he'd had all night, and pressed his face into her hair, breathing deeply.

"What's crazy?"

She turned in his arms and looked up at him, her eyes searching his. "This. The way I feel about you."

Exhilaration and regret surged through Tyler, warring within him. He was a masochist, because he couldn't help asking. He had to know.

"How do you feel?"

She made a sound that was half laugh, half groan, and bent her head to his chest. "Like I have the flu; I'm hot and shivery all at the same time, and whenever I'm near you I can't seem to think straight."

"Hey," he said softly, and put a finger beneath her chin. "Look at me."

She raised her head. Her eyes were dark pools in the pale oval of her face.

"Whatever you have, it must be catching."

Then he bent his head and covered her mouth with his.

CHAPTER ELEVEN

A S KISSES WENT, it was as about as perfect as Callie could have imagined. His lips were warm and firm, and moved with sensual slowness over hers. He shifted slightly, and cupped the back of her head with one big hand, his fingers sliding through her hair to gently massage her scalp.

Callie was helpless to prevent the small sound of pleasure that escaped her, and she pressed closer to Tyler, wanting more. He slanted his mouth across hers, and she opened for him instinctively, welcoming the hot, silky intrusion of his tongue. He tasted of sweet tea, and she angled her face to give him better access. He immediately deepened the kiss, fusing his mouth to hers, and stroking her tongue with his own until hot coils of desire unfurled low in her abdomen.

Wreathing her arms around his neck, Callie pushed her fingers through his short hair, reveling in the velvet-rough texture. He made a sound of approval, and then dragged his mouth from hers. He tipped her face to one side and pressed heated kisses along her jaw, to the sensitive spot below her ear, before taking the delicate lobe between his teeth.

Callie moaned softly.

The sensation of his tongue as it followed the whorl of her ear sent a sharp knife of pure need straight through her. In answer, Tyler moved his lips along the side of her neck to where she knew her pulse beat erratically. Her breathing was coming fast, and she stroked her hands over the wide breadth of his shoulders, urging him closer.

"Christ, you smell delicious," he muttered against her skin. "I want to eat you."

"That—that sounds good," she managed, her voice sounding strangled.

He laughed softly, and then he was kissing her again, more urgently now. His hands roamed across her back, and down over her bottom, lifting her up against his hips so she could feel how hard he was. His hands kneaded her cheeks beneath the thin fabric of her dress, and it was all Callie could do not to push against him, to beg him to touch her where she needed it most. She burned for him.

He felt amazing beneath her hands, all hard bone and muscle. But when she pushed her fingers beneath the soft material of his shirt, his skin was like hot silk.

"I love touching you," she panted, when she could catch her breath.

"Same." He growled softly, and claimed her mouth in a kiss so searing Callie thought she might spontaneously combust.

As to prove his point, he put a hand at the small of her back to anchor her against him, and cupped one breast with his free hand. Callie gasped, and then arched into his palm. Beneath the cotton dress, her nipple tightened, sending a reflexive jolt of lust to her sex. He found her nipple and gently rolled it between his fingers until Callie whimpered softly against his mouth.

"Good?" he asked.

She made in an inarticulate sound of assent, and then his hand moved lower, beneath the hem of her dress. Callie could feel the hard calluses on his palm as it skated over her bare thigh, and then he was cupping her intimately, the fragile barrier of her panties no match for his lean fingers.

"Oh, man," he said, and his voice sounded choked. "You are so freaking soft."

Callie knew she should stop him. This was too much, too soon, but every cell in her body ached for more, so instead of pushing him away, she shifted her weight to provide him better access. His fingers slid beneath the fabric, and then he was touching her, parting her. She clutched at his shoulders, almost unable to bear the touch of his fingers against her sensitized flesh.

"Please," she managed, "I can't take it."

She didn't know if she was begging him to stop, or continue, but she almost wept in disappointment as his fingers ceased their magical exploration and he withdrew his hand. He wrapped his arms around her, holding her tightly. Callie realized she was trembling. She felt hot and achy and unfulfilled, and everything in her cried out for him to finish what he'd started…to provide her with the release she so desperately needed. She dragged in several deep breaths in an effort to calm herself.

"Sorry," she finally managed to say, her words muffled against his shoulder.

He pulled back slightly and cupped her face in his two hands. Callie gazed up at him, feeling bemused and a little desperate for more of his touch. His expression was tight, as if he were in pain.

"Why are you sorry?" he asked, stroking her cheek with his thumb. "One of us has to think straight, and clearly it wasn't going to be me."

"You didn't seem to have any problem stopping," she complained.

He traced her mouth with his finger. "You said you couldn't take it, so I stopped. No means no, right? I'd never do anything you weren't ready for."

She knew he was aroused; had felt the evidence of it when she'd pressed against him, and yet he'd put the brakes on for her. Unless she'd misread him, and he wasn't as into her as she'd thought.

As if reading her mind, he tipped her face up so he could search her eyes.

"Listen," he said. "Just so there's no misunderstanding, everything in me wants to take you someplace quiet and spend about the next two weeks getting to know every inch of you."

Callie knew what was coming next.

He drew in a deep breath. "But that wouldn't be fair to you, because I'm heading out tomorrow. Besides which, you're going through a lot right now with your dad in the hospital, and the fire destroying your home." He hesitated. "I'd feel like I was taking advantage of you."

Realistically, she knew he was right. No matter how gorgeous and sexy she found him, she'd be making a huge mistake to let their attraction for each other go any further. The likelihood of their seeing each other again was slim to none, and she wasn't accustomed to one-night stands, which is what sleeping with Tyler would amount to.

"You're right," she conceded reluctantly.

"Yep." He sounded as disappointed as she felt, which made her feel marginally better. "C'mon, I'll walk you back to your cabin."

He scooped up both pairs of boots in one hand, and kept his arm around her shoulders as they made their way across the field. He steered her past the groups of people sitting around the low-burning campfires, and the incident command tents, where emergency responders were still coordinating fire suppression efforts. When they reached her cabin, she stood on the first step of the small porch, and turned to look at him.

"Thank you for everything, Tyler."

He was eye-level with her now, and he reached out to tuck a strand of her hair behind one ear. "You're a pretty amazing lady, you know that? I'm sorry we couldn't have met under different circumstances, but I'm not sorry we met."

"Me, either. Take care of yourself, okay?"

Leaning forward, he kissed her sweetly, breaking away before it became heated. He handed her the boots, stroked his thumb across her mouth, and turned and walked away. Callie watched him go, feeling bereft. He looked back once, an expression of regret on his face. Callie went inside the cabin where she leaned against the closed door and shut her eyes. Had she just made the biggest mistake of her life in letting him go? She couldn't remember the last time anyone had made her feel the way he did.

Alive.

Sexy.

With a groan of regret, she pushed away from the door and crossed the small living room to the bedroom at the back of the cabin. Fumbling in the dark, she found the bedside lamp and turned it on low. The light cast a soft glow on the honey-colored log walls, and the bed looked inviting with its pretty quilt and plump pillows. She was just reaching for the zipper at the back of her dress, when she heard a knock on the cabin door.

Her heart leapt inside her chest. She opened the door, and there he stood. Her heart beat so hard she was sure he must hear it. They stared at each other for several long seconds, and then he held up the sweater she'd brought with her earlier.

"You forgot this," he said.

"That's not all I forgot." Reaching out, she caught his wrist and pulled him inside the cabin, and shut the door. Pushing him up against the planks, she thought she saw surprise, and then relief in his eyes. "I forgot that I'm not ready to say good-bye to you. Not yet."

TYLER HAD HOPED something like this might happen, but when Callie dragged him into her cabin, and planted a searing kiss on him, he couldn't hide his relief or his satisfaction.

He caught her in his arms, letting the sweater drop to the floor, forgotten. If she'd been sexy before, now she was like a living flame in his arms. Her hands curled into his shirt as she kissed him, deeply.

"I want this," she gasped, between kisses. "Don't try to change my mind."

"Okay." Tyler couldn't help but smile, scraping his teeth against hers as she smiled back. "I won't."

Before she could protest, he lifted her in his arms and carried her to the small bedroom, and set her on her feet beside the bed.

"You have no idea how hard it was for me to let you go, earlier," he confessed, sliding one hand beneath her hair and framing her jaw in his hand. "But I didn't plan this. When I saw your sweater on the chair, I really just meant to return it to you."

"I believe you," she said softly, and leaned up to kiss him, tracing her tongue lightly along his lips.

It was all the invitation Tyler needed. With a groan, he deepened the kiss, slanting his mouth over hers, and pushing his tongue against hers. Her lips were incredibly soft and she tasted like the lemonade she'd had earlier, by the fire. Even the knowledge he was behaving like a complete hypocrite, since he was leaving tomorrow, couldn't diminish the lust that swamped him.

Right now, with Callie making soft moans of pleasure as he kissed her, he couldn't think beyond this moment. It had been years since he'd had such an urgent need to see a woman spread out beneath him, and he desperately wanted to see if Callie came close to the fantasy images he had of her in his head.

He buried his fingers in her silky hair, angling his mouth across hers for deeper penetration. She made a noise of approval and stroked her tongue against his, sliding one hand to the nape of his neck. Her fingers were cool against his heated skin. Tyler dragged his mouth from hers and sucked in a steadying breath. He needed to slow down, because as much as he wanted Callie, he also wanted to savor every moment of what was to come.

"I want to see you," she whispered on a ragged exhale. "I want to see all of you."

Her dark eyes were a little hazy with pleasure, and her

mouth was moist from his kisses. Tyler immediately reached a hand behind his head and grabbed a fistful of his tee shirt, dragging it off.

"You are so beautiful," she said softly, her gaze raking over his body. She traced a fingertip over the tribal tattoo on his arm, and then down the groove that bisected his torso, admiring his pecs and stomach. "I could just look at you all day."

Tyler was under no illusions that he was the best-looking guy on the smokejumping crew. Sure, he had a great physique, honed through years of hard work and training. But some of the younger guys could probably have a successful career in modeling if they ever decided to give up firefighting. But Callie looked at him as if he really was the most gorgeous man she'd ever seen. He felt like a freaking superhero.

"You can do more than just look." He smiled, using the back of his knuckles to sweep her hair back from her face. Her expression was one of feminine desire, and Tyler felt his body harden in response. "Tell me what you want."

"I want you to kiss me again," she entreated, and reached up to wind her arms around his neck.

Tyler gave a groan of surrender and fused his lips to hers. At the same time, he bent and lifted her into his arms. She laughed as he bent a knee onto the mattress and laid her across the quilt, and then collapsed beside her, pretending to have strained himself with the effort.

"I'm just kidding." He reassured her with a grin, rolling toward her. "You don't weigh that much."

"Come here," she said and laughed.

She welcomed him into her arms as naturally as if they'd been lovers for years, although he would have staked his life on the fact that making love with a virtual stranger wasn't something Callie McLain made a habit of. Even now, as he studied her face, she swept her lashes down, hiding her eyes from him. He pressed his mouth against each fragile eyelid, hearing her uneven breathing and knowing if he slid his hand over her breast, he would feel the frantic beat of her heart against his palm. Instead, he dragged his mouth along the curve of her cheek and then teased her lips with his tongue, licking and kissing their plumpness.

With a soft gasp, she turned her head to follow the trail he made, seeking more of the sensual contact. Tyler complied, slanting his mouth across hers and kissing her deeply. She arched against him and her hands slid over his shoulders, her fingers smoothing over his back.

Rolling to his side, Tyler pulled Callie with him, one hand sliding along her hip until his fingers encountered the smooth, cool skin of her thigh. Capturing her leg, he pulled it across his hips as he continued to kiss her. She moaned and pushed closer, clutching at his back. Lust, hot and urgent, jackknifed through his gut. His cock throbbed where he pressed against her center and all he could think about was driving himself into her heat. She'd be tight and slick, and he wanted to see her lose control.

Tyler raised his head and stared down at her. The bed-side lamp bathed her skin in a warm glow. Her irises were the color of warm sherry. Right now, her eyes were cloudy with pleasure, and her pale skin had a taken on a faint flush of color. Her breathing came in soft pants against his neck, and her fingertips smoothed distracted circles over his shoulder blades.

She shifted closer, hitching her leg higher over his hip. Tyler couldn't resist sliding his hand along the silken length of her thigh until he encountered the edge of her panties. He wanted to slip his fingers beneath the elastic and stroke the soft skin of her buttocks. He wanted to push the fragile fabric aside and explore her cleft, the way he had earlier. Was she still damp with need? He ached to find out, but the last time he'd touched her so intimately, she'd panicked. So instead, he cupped her rear in his hand and kneaded the firm flesh through the satin fabric until she moaned into his mouth and pressed even closer. Despite her delicate appear-ance, she gripped him with surprising strength.

Breaking the kiss, she pulled back enough to look at him. "I want to see you."

Before Tyler could guess her intent, she pushed him onto his back and rose over him, hiking her dress over her legs as she straddled his thighs. He lay back against the pillows, watching her as she devoured him with her eyes.

"Oh, man," she said softly, smoothing her palms over his

abdomen and chest. "You're incredible. Your skin is like hot silk, but underneath you're so hard."

She had no idea.

All she had to do was glance down to see the evidence of his raging arousal. She was caressing his body, both with her hands and her eyes, tracing her fingers over his ribs and chest, and lingering on the sensitive nubs of his nipples. Her eyes reflected feminine desire, and he felt himself harden even more beneath her appreciative gaze.

How long had it been since he'd been this jacked for a woman? He'd made a mistake in coming here, he knew that. A long-distance relationship wouldn't work for them. But for the first time in years, he'd found himself fantasizing about a woman and anticipating what it would be like to fit his body to hers, to give her pleasure and absorb her soft cries as she came apart in his arms.

Now Callie's fingers traced the contours of his abdominal muscles until they reached the waistband of his pants and lingered there. Her eyes were on the unmistakable bulge behind his zipper. Her lips parted and slowly, as if afraid he might try to stop her, she laid her hand over him. Tyler groaned and barely restrained himself from arching into her palm.

Her eyes flew to his face. "May I?"

Tyler held his breath as Callie unbuckled his work belt, and then unfastened the button on his jeans. Slowly, she drew the zipper down. But when she spread the denim aside and cupped him through the thin fabric of his underwear, he nearly came off the mattress. He wanted to turn her beneath him on the bed, drag her panties off, and bury himself in her heat. Instead, he bent his arms behind his head and let her do as she pleased, although it was more difficult to control his ragged breathing and hammering pulse.

"I want to undress you," Callie said, and scrambled off the bed to pull his boots off, dragging his socks with them. Then she climbed back over him on all fours, until her hands were braced on either side of his head and her dark hair hung around their faces like a curtain. She fixed her gaze on his mouth before slowly lowering her head and covering his lips with her own.

Tyler had intended to let her take the lead and set the pace, but her kiss was like a drug, sucking his willpower out of him and making rational thought almost impossible. With a deep groan of surrender, he caught her face in his hands, thrusting his fingers into the cool, silky mass of her hair and deepening the kiss. Callie lowered herself onto him, until her breasts pressed against his chest and the ridge of his erection strained against her center.

"You feel so good," he muttered against her mouth. When she slid experimentally along the length of his rigid cock, he gave a hiss of pleasure and reached down to grip her hips and guide her movements.

"Ohmigod." Callie breathed, and settled herself more fully against him.

Tyler slid his hands beneath her skirt and cupped her rear, stroking and squeezing her pliant flesh. She gasped into his mouth and her movements became more urgent. Reaching between her shoulder blades, Tyler found the zipper at the back of her dress and drew it down until the fabric gaped away from her body and he could see her pink-tipped breasts.

Tyler broke the kiss and pushed her to a sitting position. Hooking his fingers in the straps of her dress, he pulled them downward. The bodice caught briefly on her nipples, and then fell in a soft whisper of fabric around her waist. Tyler let his breath out and covered her breasts with his hands, testing their weight and gently kneading them. They were just large enough to fill his palms, and he rubbed his thumbs across the distended tips, hearing her soft hum of pleasure.

"Take this off," he commanded softly.

Callie complied, pulling the dress over her head before she tossed it onto the floor. Just as he'd imagined, she was slender and pale, her skin flawless. She looked at him through hazy eyes, and caught his hands in hers, pulling them back up to cover her breasts.

"Touch me," she breathed. "I want to feel your hands on me."

With a soft growl, Tyler sat up and wrapped his arms around her as he crushed his mouth to hers, sliding his tongue along hers and feasting on her lips until he thought he'd burst with need. Her skin was warm and silken against his, and he skated his fingers over her back, exploring the dips and curves of her spine, gratified when she shifted restlessly and tried to get even closer.

"Here, let's try this," he said, and turned her onto her back. He knelt between her splayed thighs and drank in the sight of her against the pillows. With her hair spread out around her and her eyes shimmering with need, she exceeded his lustful imaginings. When her gaze dropped meaningfully to his cargo pants, he didn't pretend to misunderstand, pushing them down and off, until he was able to drop them onto the floor beside her dress.

She gave a soft "oh" of admiration, and reached out to slide her fingers beneath the waistband of his briefs and tug them down, releasing his erection. Tyler gritted his teeth as she stroked the head of his penis and then closed her hand around him, squeezing him gently. He sucked air into his lungs and struggled for control, but the sight of her slim, pale fingers around his hard length was too erotic. With a soft growl, he wrapped a hand around her wrist and pulled her away, using his free hand to shove his briefs down over his thighs. He came over her, bracing his weight on one arm as he kicked his underwear completely free. Naked, he settled himself into the cradle of her hips. She stared at him with a mixture of desire and anticipation that he found impossible to resist.

"Are you sure about this?" he asked softly, tracing his thumb over the plumpness of her lower lip. "No regrets later?"

Turning her face, she caught the pad of his thumb between her teeth and bit gently, before drawing the digit into her mouth and sucking on it. The sensation caused a white-hot bolt of lust to ricochet through his body and settle in his groin, where he pulsed hotly. Whatever illusions he'd had of letting her set the pace were obliterated with each soft, hot sweep of her tongue.

"I'm sure." She assured him, releasing his thumb and reaching for him. "Whatever happens later, I won't regret this."

Tyler grunted his approval and replaced his thumb with his mouth, kissing her so deeply that their teeth scraped together as he stroked her tongue with his own. At the same time, he slid a hand to her rear, cupping her and lifting her against his hardness.

CALLIE DIDN'T KNOW what she'd been expecting, but Tyler completely consumed her until she could no longer think straight.

"I want you inside me." She gasped against his mouth, and reached between their bodies to curl her fingers around his thick length. He made a constricted sound of pleasure and Callie felt her own desire kick into full gear as she stroked him.

"Enough"—he rasped into her ear—"or I won't last."

Tyler dragged his mouth away from hers and bent his

head to her shoulder. Callie felt him shudder lightly before he rolled to his side, pulling Callie with him.

"Take these off," he commanded hoarsely, and pushed her panties down over her hips.

Callie helped him, until she was able to kick the garment free, and then she was as nude as Tyler.

"You're so beautiful," he said hoarsely, and splayed his hand over her abdomen, just above the narrow strip of curls.

His palm was warm and callused against her skin, and when he slid his hand lower, she spread her thighs so he could cup her intimately. She ached with need, and pushed against his hand to tell him without words she wanted more. But when he parted her folds and slid a finger over her slick flesh, she gasped from the shock of pleasure that jolted through her.

"You are so wet," he said with a groan.

He swirled a finger over her, causing her hips to jerk, but when he inserted a finger inside her she nearly came off the mattress.

"Yes! That feels so good."

Tyler gave a groan and bent his head to cover her mouth. Callie kissed him greedily, drawing on his tongue and spearing her fingers through his hair. Tension coiled tightly inside her with each sensual stroke of his finger.

"I'm not going to last," she managed to gasp. "I want you inside me when I come."

He muttered a soft oath and reached for his pants.

"Hang on." He fished through the pockets until he found his wallet, withdrew a small foil packet, and tore it open with his teeth.

Callie watched as he covered himself, the sight of his strong hands on his erection incredibly arousing. He shifted so he came over her completely. Bracing his weight on one arm, he positioned himself at her entrance. His features were taut. His entire body was primed and ready, every muscle standing out in stark definition. Aroused, Tyler Dodson took her breath away.

He fitted himself at her opening and, with his gaze locked on her, he slowly surged forward. Callie sucked in her breath. The thick, hot slide of him inside her caused her to arch instinctively upward.

"You're so tight," he muttered. Hooking a hand beneath her thigh, he drew her leg up and over his hip as he began to move. He stretched her, filled her, eased himself into her until her buttocks were flush against his hips and there was nothing but the taste, scent, and feel of Tyler, in her and surrounding her.

"Are you okay?" he asked against her mouth.

In answer, Callie arched against him and drew both legs up until her heels rested on his firm butt. The movement opened her even more, and when she shifted her hips restlessly beneath him, he groaned and buried his face in her neck.

"I'm more than okay," she breathed against his lips, and

he plunged into her. The sensation of him filling her was more exquisitely intense than anything she had ever experienced.

"Kiss me," she begged.

He turned his face and caught her lips in a deep kiss. He drew on her tongue even as his pace quickened and he thrust into her with increasing urgency.

"Come for me," he growled, and punctuated his words with another thrust of his hips against hers.

With a choked sob, she convulsed around him as her orgasm tore through her in a blinding rush of pleasure. The intensity of her release was enough to push Tyler over the edge as well, and with a hoarse shout, he plunged into her one last time, shuddered, and went still. He dropped his head to her shoulder, and Callie hugged him against her. Their breathing was ragged and she could feel the heavy, uneven thumping of his heart against her chest. He pressed a kiss against her neck, just at the juncture of her jaw. His breath, warm and fresh, washed over her as he dragged air into his lungs.

"That was…amazing." Carefully, he withdrew from her and discarded the condom, before rolling to his side, pulling her with him and tucking her back against his chest. He dipped his head and caught her earlobe between his teeth, nipping gently before soothing the tender flesh with his lips and tongue.

Amazing didn't come close to describing what Callie had

just experienced. Simply put, the sex had been the hottest, most incredible she'd ever had. She closed her eyes. She wouldn't think about tomorrow, or all the tomorrows after that. She had tonight, and it would have to be enough.

CHAPTER TWELVE

TYLER LEFT DURING the night, kissing her sweetly and letting himself out into the dark. Callie lay awake until dawn, unable to stop thinking about him. Her body was tender in all the right places from their lovemaking, and her skin felt sensitive and abraded from the roughness of his beard. Her only regret was that she wouldn't feel like this again, maybe ever.

She told herself it wouldn't do any good to get involved with him, or even get to know him better since they lived so far apart. She had to remind herself how much she disliked the cold of Montana. And the long winter nights. And the isolation. California was where she wanted to be. She could never be happy in Montana.

Really.

No matter how beautiful it was, or how good it felt to be back.

She lay curled on her side with the pillow bunched beneath her cheek. His scent still clung to the sheets, and she breathed deeply. He would leave St. Mary that day, and she'd probably never see him again. The thought was so depressing; she nearly dragged the covers over her head.

She didn't regret sleeping with him, even though she'd never done anything so daring or out of character in her entire life. She'd thought she might feel guilt or shame, but there was only disappointment they wouldn't share the experience again. He'd been an amazing lover, both tender and strong, seeming to understand what her body craved even when she didn't. If anything, the intensity of her own response to him was what bothered her the most. Her lack of inhibitions was almost embarrassing, in retrospect. She'd never considered herself to be passionate, but he'd brought out a side of her she hadn't known existed.

She'd had relationships before, but none of her former partners had been able to wring the cries of pleasure from her that Tyler had. Just thinking about it made her body go hot all over.

With a groan, she swung her feet out of bed and took a lukewarm shower in the tiny bathroom, before pulling on a pair of jeans and a cotton blouse. She pushed her feet into her boots, scooped her hair back into a ponytail, and grabbed her small backpack. She didn't want to think too much about Tyler, because if she did, she'd have to admit last night had been a mistake. She'd thought she could sleep with him without becoming emotionally involved, but every time her thoughts turned to him, her chest ached, and she felt a little hollow inside.

When she stepped out of the cabin, she immediately

looked toward the spot where the Glacier Creek smokejump-ers had made their camp, but they had already packed up their gear and left. Only the flattened grass provided any evidence that they had been there at all. In fact, she saw many of the emergency responders were pulling down their tents, and loading their equipment into the trucks.

While she knew this was a positive sign, because it meant the wildfire was finally under control, she couldn't help but feel bereft. Where was Tyler now? At the small airfield, preparing to return to Glacier Creek?

Callie walked across the campground to where the emer-gency animal rescue center had been set up. Already, many of the animals had been claimed by owners or, like the rescued deer, had been returned to the wild.

Two volunteers were already there, and together they helped Callie provide the animals with their daily treatments. She noted with satisfaction that Napi was growing stronger and his bite wound was healing nicely. Even his burns were improving, and if his happiness at seeing her was any indica-tion, he was feeling better, too.

"Have we had any reports of a missing dog?" she asked Kim, one of the volunteers.

"Nothing yet. We've posted pictures locally, and the newspaper is going to run a short article about the animals that have come in." She held a cat that had been brought in with a burned tail, and now she rubbed her finger under the animal's chin, eliciting a purr. "Hopefully they'll all find homes before too long."

Callie bent and gently stroked Napi, thinking if nobody came forward to claim him, perhaps he would make a good companion for her father, once he left the hospital. Reassuring herself the animals were in good hands, she climbed into the kennel truck and drove to Browning. It was still early when she peeked in at him, but Frank McLain was sitting up in his hospital bed, eating his breakfast.

"Hey, Dad," she said, as she pulled up a chair and surveyed his breakfast tray. "What is it this morning?"

He grimaced. "Oatmeal. Always oatmeal."

"Well, I hate to be the one to break it to you, but your days of steak and eggs are probably over."

"Hmph. When are they going to let me out of here? I need to see my wolves, make sure they're okay."

"I know, Dad." She tried to sound reassuring. "But first you need to get better. The doctors think you'll be able to leave by the end of the week, but they want you to go to rehab."

He grimaced. "Why would I do that?"

"It would only be until you get your strength back, maybe another week or so. You've been through a lot."

"I feel fine."

His color was better, but Callie thought he looked tired and drawn. Besides, with no home to return to, rehab would give her some time to persuade him to come back to Monterey with her.

"Listen, Dad, since you're feeling better…" She paused, and clasped her hands together in her lap, not sure how to continue. "There's something I need to talk to you about."

"I know about the house."

Her head snapped up. "You do?"

"One of the firefighters came to see me this morning." He pushed the tray table away, and his eyes grew suspiciously bright. "He said the house was destroyed, but the wolves survived. Except for Nina. But she was an old girl, and the stress of the fire was probably too much for her."

Callie leaned forward. "A firefighter came to see you? Today?"

"About an hour ago. Nice young fella, said he was a friend of yours."

"Tyler Dodson."

"That's him." He sighed deeply and folded his hands across his blankets. "So I've been thinking that if the wolf enclosures are still intact, maybe I could get a trailer and haul it up there. That way I could still stay on the property."

"Dad. No, just…no. That's not going to be possible." She swiped a hand across her eyes. "The wolves have been placed at other sanctuaries."

"But that's just temporary. As soon as I'm better, I'll go get them."

Callie felt an overwhelming surge of frustration. This was the way it had always been with her father—the wolves came first. Always the wolves. She'd gone into veterinary medicine because she cared about animals, too, so she got it. She understood his concern for them, but this was too much.

"Dad," she said, her throat tightening, "you're not getting those wolves back. That was part of the deal. They've been placed permanently at other sanctuaries in Missoula and Wyoming, and that's the end of it."

His bushy brows drew together. "It doesn't have to be. I'll bring them back."

Callie pushed her chair back and stood up. "Do you realize how close you and I came to dying in that wildfire? Do you? All because you cared more about those wolves than you did about your own safety." She paused. "Or mine."

He looked stricken.

"It's true," she continued, unfazed by his apparent dismay. She'd harbored her own hurt and resentment for too long. "Your refusal to leave because of the wolves nearly got us both killed. All my life, you've put those animals before your own family. But now your family is gone, your house is gone, and you can't return to that property."

She waited for him to respond, but he was silent, staring at her as if he'd never seen her before.

She leaned forward. "The sanctuary is gone, Dad, and you have to accept it. You have to start thinking about what you're going to do for yourself. Just Frank McLain. No wolves, no sanctuary, just you."

"That sanctuary *was* my life. I don't know what else to do." He bent his head. "I don't even know how to be a father."

Callie leaned forward. "Then come to Monterey and live with me."

His expression was one of shock. "What?"

"I have plenty of room, and it would be nice to have you close."

"California?" he asked in dismay. "No, never. I'll never leave Montana. This is my home."

Callie had expected him to say this, but the knowledge he'd prefer to stay where he had nothing, rather than come live with his only daughter, was hurtful.

"I dropped everything to be here with you," she said carefully. "I left my home, my job, and basically put my life on hold. I did it because I love you, and because you needed me. I've never asked you for anything. But I'm asking you now. Come to Monterey. Do this for me."

His chin wobbled as he stared at her, and for a moment Callie thought he might actually cry.

"It's true I haven't been much of a father," he finally said and his voice shook. "But I always expected you to leave, just like your mother did. I guess it was easier for me not to get too close, knowing that day would come. And it did."

Callie gave him a tolerant look. "That's a poor excuse, Dad. I was a child. You had me for thirteen years before mom left, and five years afterwards, and I don't remember there being any difference in our relationship." She leaned forward and looked into his eyes. "In spite of my efforts."

To her astonishment, he reached out and gripped her hand. "I've never been good when it comes to feelings, and talking about stuff. I don't know why, that's just the way I am. Maybe that's why I prefer the company of animals. They don't ask you to share every thought that's going through your head." He squeezed her fingers. "But I've always been proud of you, Callie. You're a good girl, and better to me than I deserve."

"Dad—"

"But I don't want to go to California." His expression softened. "All my memories are here. I've lived here my whole life. This is where I belong. I'd be like a fish out of water out there."

Callie felt herself relenting. This might be the most heartfelt conversation she'd ever had with her father.

"Who will look out for you?" she asked. "I'd worry about you, so far away."

One corner of his mouth lifted in the semblance of a smile. "You could move back to Montana. After all, this is where you were born."

Callie opened her mouth to protest, but he stopped her.

"Just think about it, okay?" His eyes were pleading. "I seem to recall you were a pretty happy kid, and you liked nothing better than being outdoors, under all that big sky."

Callie had a swift recollection from her childhood, of a summer day spent hiking through the mountains with her father as he'd pointed out the various animal tracks they'd encountered, and talked about the wildlife in the area. He'd been a wonderful teacher.

"It was a great childhood," she admitted. "But we're not talking about me. We're talking about you."

He withdrew his hand from hers and settled back against the pillows. "I can't make any decisions right now," he said, gruffly. "But I promise to give it some thought."

"You will?" Callie couldn't keep the surprise out of her voice.

"If I can't run the sanctuary anymore, I can at least move closer to where the wolves are now. Maybe the Missoula sanctuary could use a part-time volunteer."

He closed his eyes, a clear signal he was finished talking, but Callie was too surprised by his words to do more than sit there.

"Oh, and one more thing," he said, opening his eyes. "That day we almost died?"

"Yes?"

"You're right—I was so concerned about the wolves, that I didn't realize the danger I put you in." He grunted. "I'm an old fool. Took that young firefighter to make me see sense."

Callie tipped her head. "Tyler? How so?"

"He told me that if I loved you, and wanted any kind of future with you, then I'd leave. So I did."

"Oh, Dad." Leaning forward, Callie brushed a kiss across his forehead. "I love you, too."

But he'd already closed his eyes.

Callie left the hospital, feeling lighter than she had in days. Somehow, it was going to work out. Glancing at her watch, she saw it was close to ten o'clock, and despite the morning's stress, she was hungry. On impulse, she drove over to the Muddy Moose Café, a sprawling log cabin style structure and one of the few breakfast and lunch restaurants in the area.

The parking lot was full, and Callie could see most of the trucks belonged to the firefighters and local responders. The thought of eating breakfast surrounded by all those people almost changed her mind, but then her stomach growled, reminding her she hadn't eaten since the previous night. Her only other option was the hospital cafeteria, and she wasn't sure she could stomach another meal from there.

Pushing through the front doors of the café, she could see at least two dozen firefighters inside, all of them scarfing down huge platefuls of eggs and pancakes and bacon. Lots of bacon.

Callie stood for a moment, looking for an open seat at the long counter, or a small table away from the noisy group, when she saw a face she recognized.

Ace saw her at the same time, and gave her a cheerful wave. The entire table of eight men turned to look at her. Callie was debating leaving when Tyler suddenly stood up. Callie's heart leapt at the sight of him. He carried his plate and a mug of coffee over to a small table near the soaring stone fireplace that dominated the room, and beckoned

Callie to join him.

"What are you doing here?" she asked, as she hooked her backpack over the chair, and sat down.

The expression in Tyler's eyes as he smiled at her was warm and intimate, and conjured up erotic images of last night.

"Our jump plane has a flat tire, so we're just waiting for the mechanic to make the repairs. The boss told us to grab some breakfast, so here we are." Pushing his plate aside, he leaned forward, crossing his arms on top of the table. The movement caused his shirt to pull tight across his shoulders and biceps, emphasizing his muscles. "How are you, Callie? Doing okay?"

Callie's mouth was dry. He looked amazing, as if he hadn't been awake for half the night, doing sexy things with her.

"I'm fine." She assured him. "Happy to see you." Impulsively she reached across the table and linked her fingers with his. "I didn't think I'd see you again, at least not so soon."

"Yeah, I'm happy, too."

He signaled a waitress, and Callie placed her breakfast order. Curling her hands around a steaming mug of coffee, she watched as Tyler finished eating his own breakfast.

"My dad said you went to see him this morning."

He paused, and set down his fork. "I did, yes. I hope that's okay. I wanted to see how he was doing."

"I think it was really great of you," she said. "You did me

a huge favor in telling him about his house, so thank you for that. It wasn't something I was looking forward to."

He pulled a face. "I hated to tell him, but I thought it might be better coming from me."

Callie smiled ruefully. "Why do I think you already know a little about my dad?"

"He took it pretty well, but he thinks he's going to reopen the wolf sanctuary." His face reflected his concern.

"I think he's finally accepted that's not going to happen." Callie assured him. "Even if the wildfire had never happened, one of the things I planned to do while I was here was persuade him to sell the property. His health is bad, and he's not getting any younger."

Tyler's expression was sympathetic. "So what will you do now?"

Callie shook her head. "I don't know. The doctors want to keep him for a few more days, and then send him to rehab for several weeks. After that, I'd really like him to come back to Monterey with me, so I can keep an eye on him. But I don't think he'll ever leave Montana. The good news is that he's finally ready to talk about the options."

"What about his property?"

"I won't sell it without his permission, but I can't imagine anyone wanting to buy the land now, not when the fire destroyed everything that made it so beautiful." She smiled brightly at him. "But that's enough about me. What about you? How long will you be in Glacier Creek?"

He looked down at their linked hands and stroked his thumb over her wrist. The contact sent a frisson of awareness through Callie. Her heart ached as she watched him, knowing this might be the last time they would see each other.

"We'll go back to the base to grab new chutes and supplies," he said, "and then we're heading west, to help contain a wildfire about two hundred miles away, on the Canadian border."

"Is there any chance you'll be coming back through St. Mary on your way home?"

"No, it's unlikely. Now that the main fire has been contained, the local crews can handle it. I don't see it flaming into a massive wildfire again."

Across the room, someone shouted his name. They both looked up, and Callie saw his boss, Captain Gaskill, gesture toward the door. The rest of the crew were already making their way out of the cafe.

"I guess that's my cue," he said with a brief smile, but Callie thought his voice sounded bleak. Standing up, he tossed some bills onto the table and came around to her side, pulling her to her feet. "I hope everything works out for you, Callie."

So this was it. Callie hated how bereft she felt at the prospect of his leaving.

"Hang on a sec," she said. Fishing in her backpack, she found a pen and scribbled her phone number and address on a napkin. She pushed it into the front pocket of his shirt.

"Just in case you're ever in Monterey."

"Come here," he said, and roughly pulled her into his arms. "Take care of yourself, Callie McLain."

Pulling back, he stared at her for several long seconds, as if memorizing her face. Then he gently brushed his thumb over her cheek, and turned away, grabbing up his hardhat before following the rest of his crew out the door.

He was gone.

CHAPTER THIRTEEN

ONE MONTH HAD passed since Tyler had left St. Mary. Since he'd left Callie. He and his crew had battled a massive wildfire along the Canadian border for two of those weeks. Since returning to Glacier Creek, he'd jumped a couple of smaller fires, but he'd been back for over a week, and things were quiet. He'd stayed busy at the base, and after hours had hung out with the crew. There had been barbeques and fishing trips, long hours at the gym, and even longer hours spent at The Drop Zone, shooting pool and drinking beer. And even though nothing in his routine had really changed, everything seemed different. He loved his job, still couldn't imagine doing anything different with his life, but there was something missing.

He had Callie's phone number and address tucked into his wallet. Was she still in St. Mary, or had she returned to Monterey? And would there finally come a day when he didn't think about her at least a hundred different times?

A bunch of the crew had headed over to The Drop Zone pub for the evening, to shoot pool and have a few beers. Now Tyler pushed through the doors, the noise and music and smells enveloping him like a friendly embrace. He'd spent more time in this pub over the last fifteen years than he had in his own home.

The long, narrow room was filled with people, and Tyler saw that most of the jump crew were already at the bar. The fifty foot oak bar had been rescued from a former brothel in the old mining town of Taft. The tin ceilings overhead were gold, and embossed with scenes from the gold rush. The walls were hung with an assortment of firefighting posters, including one that read, *"It's not a party until the fire depart ment shows up.*" A vintage juke box cranked out country music, while two couples meandered lazily around the small dance floor. From the room at the back of the pub, he could hear the ricochet of balls as groups of people shot pool at the two tables.

He found a stool at the bar next to Vin, and ordered a beer. A baseball game was underway on the large, flat-screen TV over the bar, and Tyler absently noted the score.

"Hey," Vin said. "About time you got your ass down here."

Jake, one of the bartenders, slid a beer in front of Tyler, and he took a long swallow. Setting his glass down, he glanced along the length of the bar to see Ace and Liam chatting with a couple of pretty girls. Ace wore a T-shirt emblazoned with the words, *"The hotter it is, the quicker we come."*

"Where's Jacqui?" he asked, shifting his attention away

from the younger men.

"She had a couple of errands to run, but she should be here shortly," Vin said. "I noticed your old man is here."

Twisting on his bar stool, Tyler looked around. There were twenty or so dinner tables grouped behind him, and more than half of them were full. The Drop Zone was a popular dining spot for the locals, and Cait, the owner's daughter, did a pretty good job in the kitchen. Then he spotted his stepfather, sitting with one of his cronies in a corner. As if sensing Tyler's scrutiny, he looked up and their eyes met. Mike leaned forward and said something to his friend, and then motioned for Tyler to come join him.

"Ah, shit, here we go," Tyler muttered. "I wonder what I did now?"

"Have you been ignoring your mother?"

"Nope. In fact, I met her for lunch the other day."

"Then I can't help you, man," Vin said, slapping him on the shoulder. "Good luck."

In the firefighting community of Glacier Creek, it was no secret Tyler and his stepfather weren't on especially good terms. Most of the younger guys thought Mike was too hard on Tyler, while the older crew members thought he was setting a good example for his stepson, and turning him into a responsible man.

But Tyler had been a responsible adult for many, many years. Now he grabbed his beer and made his way through the tables to where Mike sat. On the wall behind Mike hung a sign that read, *"Firefighters can take the heat."* Mike's buddy had left, and Tyler sat down in the vacant chair, leaning back and crossing his booted feet to let Mike know he wasn't intimidated. But he'd be lying if he said his heart wasn't pounding just a little bit faster, wondering what criticism Mike would level at him this time.

"Hey, Tyler, good to see you," Mike said in greeting.

"Is it?" he asked drily.

If Mike was surprised by Tyler's acid response, he didn't show it. He curled his hands loosely around his own beer, considering him through narrowed eyes.

"I haven't seen you in a while. But I heard what you did out in St. Mary, helping to save that family and their animals."

Tyler shrugged. "Just part of the job."

"Sam called me when you went into the hospital. I would have come out, but he said you'd probably get released before I arrived."

Uncrossing his feet, Tyler scooted his chair forward and leaned in. "Really? You would have come out to see me? Why?"

Now Mike did look surprised. "Why wouldn't I? Of course I would come; you're my—" He broke off, as if realizing what he'd been about to say.

"*Your son?* Is that what you were going to say?" Tyler gave a snort of disdain. "Because I seem to recall you telling me that I *wasn't* your son."

Mike frowned. "When did I say that?"

Tyler gave a disbelieving laugh. "Are you kidding me? Those were almost your first words to me after you and mom got married."

Mike grew quiet. "I'm sorry, Tyler. I don't remember saying that to you."

Now it was Tyler's turn to be surprised. "I was five years old. I was so excited that Mike Eldridge—the bravest smokejumper around—was going to be my father, and then you just crushed me."

Mike raised his eyebrows and then blew out a hard breath. "Wow. I don't know what to say."

Emboldened, Tyler leaned forward. "Did I do something to disappoint you? Is that why you never let me get close to you; why you always stayed aloof?"

Mike's expression registered his shock. "Is that what you think?"

Tyler spread his arms wide. "What else would I think? I tried so hard to get your attention—your approval. I pretty much excelled at everything, and you never even acknowledged it."

"You have to understand that your father was my good friend. My best friend. And how did I repay his friendship? I married his widow." His voice carried a wealth of self-recrimination. "I loved your mother—I still do. But don't you think I felt guilty for stealing my best friend's girl?"

Tyler stared at him. "You didn't steal her—he was dead.

He'd been dead for three years when you married mom."

Mike splayed his hands. "Well, that's not how I felt. I felt like I'd somehow betrayed your father. And I decided then that I wasn't going to steal you, too. Your father was Bryce Dodson, and I promised myself I'd never let you forget that."

Tyler sat back, stunned. "You're wrong," he finally said. "I only ever had one father, and that was you. Bryce Dodson may have been my biological father, but you raised me."

Mike looked quickly away, out over the dance floor, but Tyler didn't miss the suspicious brightness to the older man's eyes, or the faint tremble of his chin. When he looked back, he smiled at Tyler. "Thank you, Tyler. You don't know what that means to me. For what it's worth, I couldn't be prouder of you than if you really were my son. In fact, I haven't thought of you as a stepson in many, many years. And when I see the fine man you've become, I know Bryce would be proud, too."

The sudden surge of emotion caught Tyler off guard, and now it was his turn to look away, and pretend that Mike's admission didn't make him feel more than a little sentimental.

"Thank you," he said simply.

They sat for several minutes, drinking their beer and pretending to watch the ballgame on the overhead flat-screen.

"So, what's this I hear you met someone out in St. Mary?"

Tyler swiveled his attention back to Mike. "Is that what they're saying?"

Was it his imagination, or was Mike's mouth curved in a satisfied smile. "That's exactly what they're saying. Well, that and the fact that since you left St. Mary, you've been as distracted and moody as a pregnant woman in her third trimester."

Tyler made a growling sound. "I'm not *moody*. I'm...conflicted."

"About what?"

Later, Tyler couldn't believe he had opened up to Mike about Callie. But he told him everything, leaving out only the details of their night together. He didn't know what he was expecting in the way of advice, especially from a hardass like Mike Eldridge, but the old man surprised him.

"Listen, son," he said carefully. "If there's one thing I've learned during my time on this earth, it's that the biggest regret is wondering what might have been."

"I tried marriage once, and it was a disaster. But if I want Callie in my life, eventually it's going to come down to marriage—that's just the kind of girl she is. I don't know if I can do that again."

Mike leaned forward. "You were both too young. I know I was hard on you back then, but all I could see was you throwing your life away on a girl you didn't really love."

That surprised Tyler. "You don't think I loved Alicia?"

"Not one whit." Mike shrugged. "You loved her just fine

with your body, just not with your heart."

"So how do I know it's not the same with Callie?"

This time, Mike didn't hide his satisfied smile. "Because it's been a month since you've seen her, and you've been moping around here like a lovesick teenager ever since. You have her number? Call her. Tell her how you feel." Mike stood up and laid a hand on Tyler's shoulder. "Your mother said you should come for dinner next Wednesday. I'd like that, too."

Tyler watched him leave. Several minutes later, Vin slid into the chair opposite. His expression was one of interest and concern. "So? How'd it go?"

"Strange," Tyler admitted. "Very strange, but in a good way."

Vin's eyebrows went up. "Really?"

"Hey, tell me something—have I been moody lately?"

Vin stood up and backed away. "Whoa, bro. I am so not going there. Just tell me one thing—did you screw up?"

Tyler thought about Callie, and how much she'd been in his thoughts during the past month. He thought about her father, and wondered if she'd found a place for him to live. Had she returned to California, or was she still in St. Mary? These were the same questions that had been plaguing him since he'd returned to Glacier Creek. So maybe Mike was right. Maybe Tyler should give her a call. If she didn't want to see him, or wasn't willing to work something out, then at least he could say he'd tried. Had he screwed up?

Big time.

TWO MORE DAYS passed before Tyler gathered enough courage to call Callie. Two days where he sometimes felt as if he'd wandered into an alternate universe. He saw Mike Eldridge frequently at the smokejumper base, and it wasn't that Mike treated him any differently than he had before—he didn't. But everything had changed, because now Tyler knew how Mike really felt.

He was at The Drop Zone, sitting at the bar. He and some of the other guys had grabbed a burger and then shot some pool. With the last game over, the guys had drifted back to the bar, and Tyler stepped outside where it was cooler and quiet.

Pulling out his wallet, he withdrew the slip of paper with Callie's information, and punched the number into his cell phone. His heart was beating a little faster than it should. The phone rang several times and then went to her voicemail. Disappointed, Tyler hung up without leaving a message. He glanced at his watch. It was almost 11 p.m., which meant it was almost 10 p.m. in California, if that was where she was.

Tapping the phone against his thigh, he thought again of her beautiful eyes, her glossy hair, and how smart and passionate she was. Had he really thought she would be hanging around, waiting for him to call? He felt like an ass. A beautiful woman like Callie was probably out doing what pretty California girls did on hot summer nights.

At that moment, his cell phone rang and he had an instant surge of hope and anticipation, quickly dashed when he realized it was the base dispatcher, recalling all the smoke-jumpers back to the base.

They had another wildfire to jump.

CHAPTER FOURTEEN

C ALLIE SAT AND stared at her cell phone.

Tyler had called, and she'd missed it. She'd gone to bed early the night before, leaving her cell phone in her pocketbook in the kitchen. She'd never even heard it ring. She'd only realized he'd called when she'd pulled her phone out to call her mother, and realized there was a missed call.

He hadn't left a message.

Was he okay?

Did he miss her?

He had tried to call her.

She turned the phone over in hands that trembled. Knots twisted in her stomach. It had been a month since she'd seen him. She'd thought of him so many times during those weeks, but had decided he was right—it could never work between them.

She'd returned to Monterey last week, after spending an additional three weeks in St. Mary. Her father had gone into a rehab facility, and Callie had spent most of her time trying to persuade him to return with her to Monterey. There had been mountains of insurance paperwork to complete, related to the loss of his house and the damage to his property. She'd been exhausted and frustrated, when help had arrived in the most unexpected way.

Callie's mother had arrived in St. Mary, and told Callie to go home, that she would take care of everything.

"But, Mom," she'd argued, "you haven't even talked to dad in years. Why would you do this?"

"Because I love you," she'd said. "And because you have a job you need to return to, and I have my summers off. And because like it or not, Frank is going to listen to me."

She almost felt sorry for her father, because when Nancy McLain set her mind to something, there wasn't much that could stop her. Seeing her parents together again also brought back all the unpleasant memories from her childhood, when their marriage was falling apart. They had avoided each other as much as possible, and when they were together, they inevitably argued.

They still argued, but Frank seemed to relish their encounters, and it hadn't escaped Callie's notice he capitulated to Nancy's demands almost too easily. She had returned to Monterey with mixed feelings, hoping her parents didn't end up killing each other—or getting back together. She wasn't sure which would be worse.

In the end, Frank had decided to relocate to Missoula, and volunteer part-time at the wildlife sanctuary where his wolves had been permanently resettled. That way, he could still be involved with them, but without the stress of managing the sanctuary. This worked perfectly for Callie, since he would also be close to a hospital and other services. Nancy had promised to remain in Montana until he found an apartment.

A cold, wet nose nudged her hand and Callie dragged her thoughts away from her parents, to the dog that stood wagging its tail and looking at her expectantly, as if to remind her she was still holding the phone.

"Hey, Napi," she said to the dog, gently stroking his head. "Should I call him back? Hmm?"

Napi whined softly and licked her hand. Callie had decided to adopt him, after nobody had come forward to claim him. His injuries had healed nicely, and his fur was beginning to grow back. He was a sweet boy, and Callie didn't regret her decision to bring him back to California with her.

"Okay, I'll call," she said, and hit the redial button before she could change her mind. Her pulse kicked up a notch, anticipating hearing his voice, but the phone just rang and rang, and then finally went to voicemail.

You've reached Tyler. Leave a message.

The sound of his deep voice brought all the memories of him rushing back, and Callie disconnected without leaving a message. She scrubbed her hands over her face, feeling inexplicably depressed. How often had she thought of him during the past four weeks?

Every day.

Every hour.

She'd thrown herself into her work at the clinic, and took Napi for long walks in the evenings. She avoided spending too much time alone in her townhouse, which suddenly felt too large, and too empty. She thought she'd be happy to return to Monterey, but for the first time since she'd moved to California, she found herself missing Montana.

Up until her parents split, her childhood had been pretty idyllic, and she had loved the winters spent ice fishing, or skiing or sledding with her friends. She missed the beautiful, balmy summers spent hiking through the park and swimming in the clear mountain lakes.

In fact, if she were honest with herself, it was only after her mother left Montana that her memories became less than idyllic, and that was because her father had been so unhappy. She missed Montana. She missed the landscape, the weather, and the people. But most of all, she missed Tyler.

She spent too much time watching the news reports and keeping tabs on the numerous wildfires around the country, in case there might be some mention of the Glacier Creek smokejumpers. But there were so many wildfires raging around the country, he could likely be anywhere.

Even California hadn't escaped what was quickly becoming the worst wildfire season in decades, with numerous fires cropping up around the state. The news didn't surprise Callie. Monterey was in the middle of one of the hottest summers on record. The air-conditioning ran constantly, and even nightfall brought little relief from the relentless heat. It was no wonder there were so many wildfires, with the soaring temperatures and shifting winds.

Callie had spent the last four days listening to the news reports about a massive wildfire in the Big Sur region, less than thirty miles from Monterey, which had already consumed more than five thousand acres and destroyed a dozen homes. Glancing at her watch, she saw it was still early, barely six-thirty. She didn't need to be at the clinic until nine o'clock.

She made herself a cup of coffee and carried her mug and her cell phone into the living room to turn on the TV and see what was happening with the fire. She wasn't concerned for her own safety; Monterey wasn't in any danger, but she couldn't recall a time when a wildfire had occurred so close to the city. Having witnessed firsthand the devastation they wrought, her sympathy went out to the residents who had been forced to flee the region, and whose homes had been destroyed.

When her cell phone rang, her heart leapt. But it was her mother on the other end.

"Are you watching the news?" she asked, without preamble.

"I just turned it on," Callie replied. "Why are you calling so early?"

"Turn it to the local channel."

Callie did, and her mouth fell open when she saw the

coverage of the Big Sur wildfire.

"Oh, my God," she breathed. "They're not containing that wildfire; it's getting worse."

"They've called in more than a thousand firefighters, Callie. I'm concerned for you."

"No, mom, don't be." She leaned forward to watch more closely. "The fire is still more than thirty miles away. It won't reach Monterey."

"That's what your father said about the Lincoln Pass fire, and his house was destroyed."

Callie frowned. "Yes, mom, I know. I was there. But this is different."

"I just want you to be prepared, in case you need to leave. Don't wait, darling."

"No, I won't." Callie assured her. "Mom, do you know if any of the Montana hotshots or smokejumpers have been sent to Big Sur?"

"I know the reporters said six hotshot crews from around the country had been called in, but I don't know if any are from Montana. They didn't say anything about smokejumpers."

"Okay. Listen, I have to go. I need to get ready for work."

"Just be safe, okay?"

Callie hung up, but instead of getting ready for work, she sat glued to the television, watching the coverage of the fire. More than one thousand firefighters had been called in, which meant this wildfire was even bigger then the Lincoln Pass fire.

Her gut told her Tyler was there. But how could she be sure? Was he safe? What if the wildfire was bigger than they could manage? Wildland firefighters died every year battling wildfires.

Snatching up her phone, Callie redialed Tyler's number. It went to voicemail again, but this time she left a message.

"Tyler, this is Callie. I'm so sorry I missed your call last night—I went to bed early and never heard the phone ring. Please call me back, okay? I need to know you're safe." She hesitated, wanting to say so much more, but in the end she chickened out. "Just…call me."

She hung up, but the news reports coming in about the Big Sur wildfire only made her feel more anxious. She knew she wouldn't be able to focus on anything until she knew he was okay.

She found the phone number for the Glacier Creek base and punched the number into her cell phone. Her pulse pounded in her ears.

A woman answered. "Glacier Creek Base Station, how may I direct your call?"

"Good morning, I'm looking for Tyler Dodson, please."

"I'm sorry, but Mr. Dodson is unavailable."

"This is Callie McLain, I'm a—a friend of Tyler's."

"How can I help you, ma'am?"

"I'm trying to find out if Tyler and his crew are battling

the wildfire at Big Sur, California."

Callie could sense the woman's hesitation. Maybe there was some kind of rule about giving out that kind of information, but Callie had to know.

"Please," she begged. "I need to know. I'm—I'm in love with Tyler. I need to know if he's safe."

There was another pause and Callie heard the woman sigh. "I know what you must be going through, truly. Yes, the crew is fighting the Big Sur fire, and have been for the past three days. But they're all safe. Try not to worry, okay? I know it's hard, but worrying won't help."

"Is there a way for me to get a message to him?" Callie asked. "I tried to call his cell phone, but it went straight to his voicemail."

"Unless it's an emergency, ma'am, I don't think—"

"This is important." Callie insisted. "I never told him how I feel, and if anything happened to him—" She broke off, unable to articulate her feelings.

"I'll see what I can do." The woman assured her. "What message would you like me to give him?"

"To just call me. Please."

She hung up, feeling emotionally wrung out. Tyler was part of the hellish scene unfolding on the television. Miles and miles of blistering flames, consuming everything in its path. Helicopters were dropping water and retardant on the fire, and several images showed firefighters desperately digging fire lines in an effort to protect homes. Callie couldn't tell if Tyler was among them.

She'd told the dispatcher she was in love with Tyler. She could argue she barely knew him, but her heart knew him. She knew everything about him she needed to know. He was strong, and tender, and had a compassionate nature he tried to hide.

She loved him.

She loved his courage and his compassion; she loved his sense of humor and his romantic streak.

And for the first time, she understood his reluctance to commit himself to her, or any other woman. Because he knew she would see these kinds of news reports and worry. For the first time, she had an understanding of what it was like to be in love with a wildland firefighter.

A smokejumper.

To worry about him, and not know if he was safe. To have her imagination run riot, creating worst case scenarios. To wonder if he would come safely home.

CHAPTER FIFTEEN

FOUR DAYS HAD passed since Callie had called the Glacier Creek Base Station and left a message for Tyler. He hadn't called her back. Callie didn't know if it was because he hadn't received the message, because he was unable to call her, or because he didn't want to call her.

She'd been awake for most of the night, watching the news coverage of the wildfire, and had fallen asleep in front of the television. The Big Sur fire had finally been contained to the degree it no longer posed a threat to the surrounding homes. The firefighters would continue to work the blaze until it was completely extinguished, but it seemed the worst was over.

After taking Napi for a quick walk, she showered and padded into the kitchen on bare feet, wearing only a thin robe, with her hair wrapped in a towel. It was Friday morning and her day off. She didn't need to be back at the clinic until Sunday morning, but she had no plans for the next two days, unless she counted food shopping.

Opening her refrigerator, she gloomily surveyed the leftovers and Chinese takeout boxes that had accumulated there.

Closing the door, she turned on the coffeemaker, and her phone began to ring.

She picked it up and looked at the display.

Tyler.

Her heart nearly exploded out of her chest as she quickly answered it.

"Tyler?"

"Hey, how are you?"

His voice was warm, and sounded so strong and healthy, Callie nearly wept with relief.

"I've been so worried about you," she confessed. "I know we haven't talked since—well, in a long time, but I've thought about you every day."

"I've thought about you, too," he said, his voice a little rougher. "I'm sorry I couldn't return your call, but things were pretty insane."

Callie waved her hand in dismissal. "No, it's fine, really. I shouldn't have called the base station, but I was just so worried about you. You're okay?"

"I'm fine. Really good."

Callie nodded, smiling, aware that her eyes had welled up. She swiped at the dampness with her free hand. "Thank goodness. Where are you now? Still in California?"

"Uh…yeah, you could say that."

Relief swamped her. "Is there any chance we can see each other before you head back? I can drive to wherever you are. I just really need to see you, Tyler." She hoped he didn't notice how wobbly her voice sounded.

"Absolutely. I need to see you, too."

Callie felt a little weak with the force of her own emotions. "Just tell me where and when."

"Why don't you open your front door?"

For an instant, her heart stopped beating, and then exploded into life. *He was here.*

She ran through the house with Napi on her heels, barking with excitement at seeing his mistress running. Callie wrenched open the front door, and there he was, still holding his phone to his ear, a silly grin on his face. He still wore his firefighting clothes, and he was covered in sweat and soot and dirt.

To Callie, he had never looked more beautiful.

She launched herself into his arms, and he caught her with a surprised laugh, his arms coming around her and holding her tight.

"Oh, Tyler," she said, and leaned back in his arms to look at him.

His eyes gleamed warmly, and his teeth were startlingly white against the black smudges on his face.

"Miss me, sweetheart?" he asked, and then his mouth came down over hers, kissing her as if he were dying of thirst, and she was a spring of cool water in the middle of a desert.

When he finally lifted his head, Callie felt dazed. He raked her with a heated gaze, taking in her toweled hair and bathrobe.

"I sure as hell hope you're naked under that robe," he said, his voice rough.

"Why don't you come inside and find out?"

She pulled him unresisting into the townhouse. As soon as the door closed, Tyler turned her against the door, pinning her there with the weight of his body. He dropped his hard hat and his gear bag onto the floor, and caught her wrists in his hands, stretching them over her head and trapping them in one of his own.

"Christ, have I missed you." He growled, and kissed her deeply.

With his free hand, he undid the sash on her robe and swept it open. Callie shivered as cool air wafted over her body, and then his hand was there, exploring her curves, cupping one breast, and gently thumbing her nipple. The last four weeks vanished, and it was as if no time had passed. He was here, and he still wanted her.

He caught her soft moan of pleasure in his mouth, stroking his tongue against hers. He could have taken her right there against the door and she would have welcomed it.

But he released her hands, and bent his head to hers, his breath coming in harsh pants.

"Baby, I want you so badly," he said. "But I am a stinking mess. I need a shower before I touch you again."

Callie laughed and leaned against him, happier than she could ever recall. "I don't mind."

He tipped her face up, and pressed his lips against the

small beauty mark beside her eye. "I mind."

She nodded and, drawing her bathrobe closed, took his hand. "Follow me."

He picked up his gear bag and followed her up the stairs to the second floor of the townhouse. Callie could have shown him the guest bathroom at the end of the hallway, but instead she drew him into her bedroom and indicated the en suite bathroom that she used.

"You should find everything you need," she said, blushing a little as his eyes swept over her bed. "Towels, soaps, and I think there's a new razor in the top drawer. Help yourself to anything."

"Thanks."

As she watched, he unfastened his suspenders and his belt, and then peeled his shirt off. Unembarrassed, Callie blatantly stared at his muscular chest and arms, and her fingers itched to explore his washboard abs, and lower.

"I don't want to drop this on your floor," he said, holding out his shirt. "It's pretty filthy."

Callie opened her closet and retrieved her small laundry basket. "Put everything in here. I'll run your clothes through the wash."

"Great. Don't go anywhere; I'll be out in just a minute."

He left the bathroom door partly open, and Callie heard the shower turn on. Napi had followed her upstairs, and now he stood at the bathroom door, whining softly.

"Sorry, buddy," Callie said, and gently led him out into

the hallway. "Go lay down. This is one time you're not invited in."

She closed the bedroom door, and then caught sight of herself in the full length mirror on the backside of the door. Her hair was still wrapped in a towel, and her face was pale except for two splotches of bright color high on her cheeks.

"Oh, my God," she muttered, and yanked the towel off, combing her fingers through her hair. She couldn't believe Tyler had seen her looking like this, and had still wanted to kiss her!

She heard him open and then close the shower door, and could picture him clearly. Suddenly, she didn't want to wait for him to finish. Pushing the bathroom door open, she was enveloped in warm steam. She slipped out of her bathrobe, and carefully approached the shower. Through the mist, she could see Tyler standing beneath the spray of water. His back was to her, and he had his face turned directly into the water as he scrubbed away the dirt and soot.

He turned as she opened the door and stepped in beside him. Her shower enclosure was generously proportioned, but he made it seem small with his height and broad shoulders. He smiled at her, water running in rivulets down his face and turning his eyelashes into wet spikes.

"I was hoping you might join me," he said, and slicked a hand over his face. "Come here."

He drew her under the spray, pulling her against him with one hand at the small of her back. He was fully aroused and the hard, hot press of him against her stomach caused an immediate rush of heat and moisture to her sex.

"I've dreamed of this," he said, his voice rough, and slid a hand beneath her hair, tipping her face up so that he could kiss her.

Callie made a soft humming sound of approval. The slick slide of his body against hers was so erotic that she couldn't wait any longer to touch him. Reaching between them, she curled her fingers around his length. He groaned and deepened the kiss.

"Oh, man, that feels too good," he muttered.

Using the fragrant shower gel, they soaped each other's bodies, exploring each other with slippery hands as they kissed, until Callie thought she would explode with need.

"I want you inside me," she said, gripping him in her hand and stroking him.

"Ah, sweetheart, I want you so badly," he said, "but there's something I've been dying to do."

Before she could guess his intent, he pushed her back against the cool tiles of the shower wall and knelt in front of her, urging her legs open with his hand.

"Tyler," she said uncertainly, her fingers tunneling through his wet hair. "I'm not sure…"

"I am," he said, and he licked her.

Callie cried out at the first touch of his tongue against her sensitive flesh and clutched at the ceramic handhold on the shower wall, feeling the world tilt around her.

He held her hips in his hands and laved her with his tongue until she came apart, pleasure washing over her in endless waves. Standing up, Tyler lifted her against the wall, his hands beneath her bottom, supporting her.

"I don't have any protection," he said, his voice hoarse with need. "But I can pull out."

Still trembling from her orgasm, Callie could hardly think straight. "No, it's okay. I'm on the pill."

"Are you sure?" His expression was taut.

"Please, Tyler."

He lowered her slowly onto his shaft, easing into her with a pained groan. "Ah, damn, you feel so good."

Callie had to agree. He filled her, stretched her, and then began to thrust into her. He bent his head to her shoulder as he moved inside her. Callie wound her arms around his neck and hung on as his movements became quicker, stronger.

"I can't last," he growled. He pushed into her one last time, his big body shuddering against hers as he climaxed.

They stood locked together for several long minutes, while Callie's heart rate returned to normal. The shower had grown lukewarm and, after a moment, Tyler let her legs slide to the floor, then withdrew from her. His breathing was still ragged as he pressed a kiss against her mouth.

"Are you okay?"

"Better than okay." She assured him. "Now that you're here."

"Let's get you warm and dry," he said.

Tyler shut the water off and reached for a towel, wrapping it around her. Stepping out of the shower, Callie felt chilled without the warmth of his body. Winding a towel around his lean hips, he stepped out after her and pulled her into an embrace.

Tipping his head down, he looked directly into her eyes. "This isn't the only reason I came here, Callie, you know that, right?"

This was the reason why women stayed with their firefighters. Tyler was tender and protective and made her feel incredibly sexy. He hadn't told her he loved her, but Callie knew their physical intimacy meant something to him.

"I think I have an idea," she replied with a smile, and traced a trickle of water where it ran down the side of his neck. "How long can you stay?"

"One of the local guys dropped me off. I can stay until tomorrow morning, and then we head back to Glacier Creek."

"Can I fix you something to eat?" She had no idea what she would make, since her refrigerator was almost bare, but guessed he was both hungry and tired. She could see smudges of exhaustion beneath his eyes.

"Sure."

In the bedroom, she pulled on a pair of loose boxer shorts and a camisole top, her standard weekend loungewear, and ran a comb through her hair.

Tyler was fishing through his gear bag, so she picked up

the laundry basket and walked to the door. "I'll wash your things. Come down to the kitchen when you're dressed."

"Thanks, babe."

Napi refused to accompany her downstairs, so she left him in the upstairs hallway and made her way down. After throwing Tyler's clothing into the washing machine, she scrounged up enough ingredients to make him an omelet. He still hadn't come downstairs, so she arranged his plate, along with a pot of coffee and a small pitcher of orange juice, on a tray and carried it upstairs.

"I've brought you some breakfast," she said, as she shouldered the bedroom door open and then stopped. Tyler lay sprawled on top of her bed, wearing a clean pair of boxer briefs, and nothing else. One arm was flung over his eyes, and she could hear his soft snores form the doorway.

"Maybe later," she said softly, and carried the tray over to one of the bedside tables, and set it down quietly.

She shook out a soft blanket and drew it over Tyler's prone body. He didn't even stir. Feeling oddly protective, Callie leaned down and pressed a soft kiss against his jaw. Then she drew the shades in the room, casting it in cool darkness, and tiptoed out of the room. He was safe and, for now at least, he was hers.

CHAPTER SIXTEEN

IF SOMEONE HAD told him five months ago he could make a long-distance relationship work, Tyler would have dismissed the notion. Back in July, he hadn't been interested in any kind of serious commitment, never mind one where he and the lady in question were separated by fourteen hundred miles.

But somehow, he and Callie had made it work. Was it ideal? Hell, no. He missed her every day that he wasn't with her, and talking with her via Skype each night only fueled the frustration he felt at not being able to touch her. But he never tired of talking with her, or listening to her stories about Napi and the veterinary clinic. He loved making her laugh, and watching her face go tender when he told her how much he missed her.

And he missed her like crazy.

They'd managed a couple of trips back and forth to see each other, and it worked in his favor that her father now lived in Missoula, which was a short two-hour drive from Glacier Creek. Callie been out to visit her father once and help get him settled into his new place. Tyler had fortunately been between calls and had managed to drive down and see her.

But now that the fire season was over, he hoped he could get back to California more frequently. The ski resort wouldn't open until December, and it was only early November. He figured he had a couple of weeks before he needed to settle in for a long, cold Montana winter. He hadn't told Callie yet, but he'd already bought airline tickets, and would head out to Monterey to surprise her in just two days. He was long overdue for some time off, and way overdue for some time with Callie.

He'd spent the morning at the base station, helping the crew install a new bathroom in the women's bunkroom. With more women joining both the smokejumper and hotshot crews, they needed the additional shower facilities. Tyler was happy for the work, as it kept his mind occupied.

He and Greg were installing three new shower stalls, and had just finished framing out the new area. Working on the construction of the showers made Tyler antsy to begin work on his timber-frame house. The foundation was in, and workers had begun raising the frame. Tyler hoped to have the house weather-tight before the winter really set in. His plan was to get most of the interior framed out during the winter, before the next fire season began. He hadn't shown Callie the new house, but he thought she would approve.

"Hey, Tyler, can you come with me for a minute?"

Tyler looked up to see Sam Gaskill standing in the

doorway. "Sure, boss," he said, setting his level down on a nearby worktable. He exchanged glances with Greg, who shrugged.

He followed Sam out of the bunkroom and toward the staircase that led to the lobby. "What's going on?"

"There's something I need you to take a look at," Sam said over his shoulder.

Perplexed, Tyler followed him down the stairs, but stopped halfway when a movement caught his attention. Callie stood in the lobby, looking up at him.

"Callie!" Pleasure surged through him. This was the last thing he had expected, especially since he had been planning to surprise *her*.

He took the stairs two at a time and caught her in his arms, hugging her tightly and laughing. "What are you doing here? Why didn't you tell me you were coming? I would have picked you up at the airport." He stood back, relishing the sight of her. "Damn, this is a surprise."

She was bundled up in a heavy, cable sweater over skinny jeans and boots, with a scarf around her neck. Her cheeks were pink from the cold, and she looked both happy and cautious.

"You're not mad that I came out without telling you, are you?"

Something in her expression caused him to pause. "That depends," he said carefully. "What's going on?"

She clasped her hands and Tyler had never seen her look

so nervous. Part of him wanted to haul her somewhere private, and kiss her until she was breathless and laughing, because her serious expression was setting alarm bells off in his head. Was she going to break up with him? End their relationship? The thought made him go cold inside.

"I have something to tell you," she said, "and I hope you won't be upset."

"Go on." He knew his tone had gone cool. She'd taken him completely by surprise. He hadn't seen this coming, and there was no way he could prepare himself.

"I am crazy about you, Tyler Dodson," she said. "Completely head over heels in love with you, and I just wanted you to know that."

Tyler's knees felt a little weak as relief poured through him. Then the impact of her words crashed over him, and he nearly stopped breathing.

She loved him.

He'd never told Callie he loved her, certain she must already know. Somehow, saying the words terrified him. But seeing the hope and love shining in her eyes, he knew he had nothing to be afraid of.

"Come here," he said roughly, and pulled her into his arms. They fit perfectly, and the feel of her body was so familiar and so comforting, that he knew he'd finally come home. He cupped her face in his hands and searched her eyes. "Baby, I love you so much. I should have told you before now. I love you with every beat of my heart."

Smiling, she turned her face and pressed a kiss into his palm. "I know you do. I knew it without you even having to say it. But I had to tell you, so that you would know."

He kissed her, a sweet fusing of their mouths that was almost reverent. "How long are you here?" he asked when they finally broke apart.

"I'm here for as long as you want."

Tyler thought about the house under construction on the north ridge. That house had been a dream of his for so long, he didn't know if he could give it up, but he knew Callie was more than just a dream; she was a dream come true.

"I want you forever," he said, his voice gruff. "If you want to live in California, then we'll do it."

Callie stared at him, her face reflecting her disbelief. "I think you actually mean that."

He nodded. "I do."

"You'd never be happy in Monterey."

"You're wrong. I'd be happy wherever we're together. I know I could get a job with the California smokejumpers, so that isn't an issue."

Callie clapped a hand over his mouth, stopping his flow of words. "Okay, well, that won't be necessary. I've had a lot of time to think about this, and I've decided I want to live in Montana. Here. In Glacier Creek."

Tyler swallowed hard, and pulled her hand away from his mouth. "Sweetheart, are you sure? You hate Montana."

"No, I don't hate Montana. I love Montana." She gestured helplessly. "I was born here. It's taken me some time to figure it out, but this is where I belong."

She sounded sincere, but Tyler was unconvinced.

"The winters are cold," he warned.

"Then you can keep me warm."

"The nights are long and dark."

She smiled. "That sounds perfectly wonderful. All the better to stay in bed."

Tyler felt something shift and ease in his chest. But there was still one more thing he had to be sure of.

"What about your job? And mine? There are times when I'm gone for weeks. How do you feel about that?"

Stepping forward, she slid her arms around his waist, and looked up at him. "I've had the last five months to get used to being without you. Do I love it? No, but I can do it. As for my job, I'm pretty sure they have veterinary clinics here in Montana."

"You'll have Napi to keep you company."

She nodded. "Yes, and I thought maybe we could get a puppy, too."

Tyler smoothed a silky strand of hair back from her face. "A puppy and maybe a couple of kids sound about right."

Later, he would tell her about the house. For now, he just wanted to let her know how much he loved her. Lowering his head, he covered her mouth, knowing he had found everything he'd ever wanted.

The End

The Firefighters of Montana

Book 1: Smolder by Tracy Solheim

Book 2: Scorch by Dani Collins

Book 3: Ignite by Nicole Helm

Book 4: Heat by Karen Foley

Book 5: Flame by Victoria Purman

Available at your favorite online retailer!

About the Author

Karen Foley admits to being an incurable romantic. When she's not working for the Department of Defense, she loves writing sexy stories about alpha heroes and strong heroines. Karen lives in New England with her husband, two daughters, and a houseful of pets.

Thank you for reading

Heat

If you enjoyed this book, you can find more from all our great authors at TulePublishing.com, or from your favorite online retailer.

TULE
PUBLISHING